ESCAPE FROM EXECUTION!

The words rang out: "Ready...aim...*fire!*"

Then the officer commanding the firing squad suddenly fell over sideways. The manhole cover he was standing on had lurched under his feet. He immediately began shouting, "Earthquake!" Earthquakes, of course, were much more usual in Central America than the sight of a big, blond American, covered with crud, popping out of a sewer with a repeating rifle in his hands, firing as fast as he could lever round after round in the chamber.

Captain Gringo mowed down the firing squad between him and the white-clad prisoner against the wall and shouted, "Sanchez! This way!" But then, when he turned to head back down the ladder into the dark tunnel, the officer was sitting up, pistol in hand, aiming the muzzle right at Gringo's head!

Novels by
RAMSAY THORNE

Renegade #1

Renegade #2: Blood Runner

Renegade #3: Fear Merchant

Renegade #4: The Death Hunter

Renegade #5: Macumba Killer

Renegade #6: Panama Gunner

Renegade #7: Death in High Places

Renegade #8: Over the Andes to Hell

Renegade #9: Hell Raiders

Renegade #10: The Great Game

Renegade #11: Citadel of Death

Renegade #12: The Badlands Brigade

Renegade #13: The Mahogany Pirates

Renegade #14: Harvest of Death

Renegade #15: Terror Trail

Renegade #16: Mexican Marauder

Renegade #17: Slaughter in Sinaloa

Renegade #18: Cavern of Doom

Renegade #19: Hellfire in Honduras

Renegade #20: Shots at Sunrise

Renegade #21: River of Revenge

Renegade #22: Payoff in Panama

Renegade #23: Volcano of Violence

Renegade #24: Guatemala Gunman

Renegade #25: High Sea Showdown

Renegade #26: Blood on the Border

Renegade #27: Savage Safari

Renegade #28: The Slave Raiders

Published by
WARNER BOOKS

Renegade #29

PERIL IN PROGRESO

Ramsay Thorne

WARNER BOOKS

A Warner Communications Company

WARNER BOOKS EDITION

Copyright © 1985 by Lou Cameron
All rights reserved.

Warner Books, Inc.
666 Fifth Avenue
New York, N.Y. 10103

 A Warner Communications Company

Printed in the United States of America

First Printing: March, 1985

10 9 8 7 6 5 4 3 2 1

El Presidente Porfirio de la Cruz Dias had ordered black coffee and hot tamales with his breakfast in bed, so he was wide awake when his bedside phone rang. But he was enjoying his hot tamales too much to answer it. The hot tamale he was eating was called Pepita. The hot tamale who was eating him was called Rosita, and she was of course being eaten in turn by Pepita, and all three of them were about to come—or at least the two young whores said they were—so the dirty old man running Mexico for his own fun and profit didn't *care* who'd called his unlisted number.

But in time all good things must end, at least until a dirty old man can get it up again. So after he'd ejaculated in the sweet little thirteen-year-old mouth of Rosita, and heard the phone still ringing, El Presidente languidly reached for the phone with one hand as he wiped his moustache with the other, and said, "Tumbe la vara, it is too early for to take calls on this line!"

The familiar voice of a trusted aide replied, "The Americano kick-in-the-balls from their embassy is making a fuss here at the office, El Presidente. He says he had a ten A.M. appointment with you and, forgive me, I mean no offense, it is quarter past eleven."

The gray-haired dictator fondled the nearest young snatch as he chuckled and said, "Show him around the garden or something. Perhaps he will find another weed for to name

1

after a gringo diplomat. Who was the idioso who named our red milkweed after himself that time?"

The aide, who was paid to know everything, said, "Poinsette, U.S. Ambassador Poinsette, El Presidente. Aside from being mad and wishing to dig up Mexican weeds, he caused no trouble. I am told they have named the spurge you speak of after him in Los Estados Unidos del Norte, and that they grow them in hot houses for to sell at Christmas time. Nobody can tell me for why. But about the Yanqui from their embassy. At the moment, he is said to be muy important and I can tell you for a fact he is muy anxious for to see you. It has something to do with that covert operation down near Progreso."

Diaz grimaced, removed his free hand from Pepita's fuzzy wet lap, and sat up straighter to say, with a sigh, "If the damned Yanqui Secret Service knows about it, it is not, by definition, a covert operation anymore. Those estupido bastards running it promised me none of the great powers would hear of it until it was a footnote of past history!"

The aide said, "If Los Yanquis know something is up, by now British Intelligence should know the whole story. What should I tell this one spilling cigar ash all over the rug outside, if you are, ah, too busy for to feed him bananas yourself, El Presidente?"

Diaz thought and said, "You'd better put him on. I know how to talk to the mother-fucking gringo shits. That is one reason I am El Presidente, no?"

There was a series of clicks at the other end of the line as the old dictator put an experimental finger in Pepita's tight anal opening. The young puta flinched and gasped, "Oh, no, por favor! I do not wish for to make love that way, Señor El Presidente!"

He growled, "You are not here for to have your own wishes come true, you stupid little peon tart. You are here for to make *my* wishes come true, and if I wish for to have you in the Greek manner you will tell me how much you love it if you wish for to leave this room alive."

Then, as she began to cry, he added, "Silencio. I must speak to another asshole, first." Then he made his voice somewhat friendlier as he explained to the upset-sounding Secret Service agent at the other end of the line, "I am so sorry to keep you waiting, my Americano friend. Important matters of state. I am sure you understand, no?"

The American he was soothing, or trying to, replied, "*No*. I've been going nuts trying to get someone down here in Red Pepperville to tell me what the fuck is going on over in Progreso!"

Diaz smiled with his voice, even though his Indian eyes narrowed, as he said, "You have found the one friend of Tío Sam who is free to tell you, then. Naturally, what I am about to tell you will go no further?"

"Just to Washington, pal. They pay us Secret Service guys to tell 'em *secrets, see?*"

"Oh, of course you will have to report this conversation to my good friends in your State Department. But I must have your word not a soul here in Mexico will hear a whisper of what I am about to confide in you, eh?"

"It's a deal. Let 'em learn their own secrets. What's the score in Progreso, Diaz?"

"What have you heard about the, ah, goings-on in Progreso, amigo?"

"Are you trying to stall me? We know the word's out that some damned body is hiring gun slicks—lots of gun slicks. So half the soldiers of fortune in Latin America are making tracks to Progreso, Yucatan, while meanwhile every fucking gunrunner with a boat that can float seems to be running guns ashore there and, even weirder, your Mexican Federales haven't made a move to stop whatever's going on. So what the fuck is going on? I'm not going to ask again, and we both know you've just asked President Cleveland for another loan!"

The Mexican leader chuckled boyishly, his face a mask a wooden Indian would be proud to manage, and replied, "Sí, old Grover is a friend of mine indeed. So I shall tell

you what is being fucked in Progreso. It is the rear
entrance of His Most Catholic Majesty, the King of Spain.
Certain other friends of mine, in the Cuba Libre Movement,
do not feel you Yanquis mean to invade Cuba at all. Most
certainly not this season at any rate. Meanwhile, Butcher
Weyler, the oddly named Spanish Military Governor of
Cuba, has been rounding up Cuban rebels, suspected
Cuban rebels, or perhaps just anyone his soldados catch on
the streets after dark, for to herd them into his no doubt
ingenious but depressing concentration camps, so—''

"So *you,* of all people, are worried about *liberty?*" The
American cut in with a knowing chuckle.

The Savior of Mexico chuckled back and confided,
"Not to the extent of granting that tedious constitucion
some of my own subjects insist on pestering me about.
But, speaking to another man of the world, man to man,
neither Mexico nor your country needs the constant brawling
in a crumbling empire right off our mutual shores, eh?
Spain is run by assholes under a king who's not even smart
enough to be called an asshole. Sooner or later the Cuba
Libre Movement has to win. Meanwhile all the fund
raising and speech making in our more sensible countries
is causing confusion among our people and extra work for
our law officers. Do you not agree that if the excitable
Cubans were not constantly plotting against the stupid
Spanish we would not be having this conversation?"

"Sure, but let's get back to Progreso."

"I have instructed my police and soldados not to go
anywhere near Progreso for the time being. The Cuba
Libre Movement is gathering an, ah, liberating army of, as
you say, gun slicks, cutthroats and otherwise useless bastards from all over, for to make a landing at some place
called the Bay of Pigs. They may know what they are
doing. Butcher Weyler may slaughter them. In either case,
both your country and mine will be ahead, no?"

The American at the other end of the line thought, then
chuckled and said, "Right. If the rag-tag invasion force

liberates Cuba we won't have to. If they fail, it'll still cost Spain and, meanwhile, you and all the other little dictators will be rid of serious gunmen your *own* rebels figure to hire for a while. Do the Spics know Mexico is allowing the Cuba Libre guys to use Progreso as a rebel base?''

Porfirio Diaz was only part Spanish, so he chose to ignore the ethnic slur as he replied, ''I doubt it. His Most Catholic Majesty can stand up, and he can piss, but not at the same time. Weyler is better at butchery than military intelligence. If he had any intelligence he might not have to butcher as many people. But if he finds out, what can he do, eh? Naturally, Mexico is officially neutral and would not dream of causing trouble for Spain. But what could I possibly do if some outlaws chose to gather in such a far-off jungle town?''

''I get the picture. Okay, it's no skin off Uncle Sam's ass, either. But just one last detail. Are you guys expecting that Yankee renegade, Lieutenant Richard Walker, the one they call Captain Gringo, to show up in Progreso?''

''I assure you, *we* are expecting *nobody* there. It was the Cuba Libre bunch, not us, who sent out the call. For why do you ask?''

''Why do I ask? Jesus H. Christ, Captain Gringo's wanted for everything but swiping Queen Victoria's opera glasses and, if they're *missing*, he probably did *that*, too! I've a dead or alive warrant on that maniac and, if he's in Progreso, why waste time trying to take anyone who's drunk the water there alive? I may need some backing from your own Rurales, though, if Walker's holed up there with friends, and—''

''Impossible!'' Diaz cut in, adding, ''You are not the only people who wish for to see Captain Gringo do the hat dance at the end of a rope. He and that little French monster he runs wild with owe me for a railroad of mine they wrecked not too long ago. But my own police are not about to accompany you into that den of thieves at Progreso and, if you will allow me to offer you some fatherly

advice, you will not try it on your own, or backed by a
platoon of U.S. Marines! Captain Gringo and his compañero,
Gaston Verrier, can produce the full effects of an army on
their own. In Progreso, at the moment, there *is* an army,
made up of the toughest professional fighting men in Latin
America, and if Captain Gringo is even there, and he may
not be, guess whose side those *other* thugs will be on!''

The Secret Service man told Diaz to let Uncle Sam
worry about that and hung up. But Diaz always worried. A
man who'd seized power after the death of Juarez and held
it with a gun ever since got good at worrying if he meant
to stay alive.

So the dirty old man, who planned on being much older
before anyone got to vote in *his* country, swung his naked
legs off the bed and told the two girls to send in his
Captain of the Guard on their way out. Then he got back
on the phone and made some important calls while he
waited. When his boss bodyguard came in to help him
wash and dress, Diaz was still fuming. He said, ''Those
fucking Yanquis are going to fuck up the whole sweet plan
if we don't stop them!''

The bodyguard moved to fill the sink in the corner with
warm water as he replied stiffy, ''Orders, my Presidente?''
But the old man just glimaced and said, ''I have already
set the wheels within wheels in motion. You just worry
about the soap and towels and, oh yes, what about my
standing orders regarding female guests to these private
quarters, Major?''

''Carried out, sir. The two girls were sent to the dun-
geons the moment they came out to tell us you were
finished with them. We thought it best to await word from
you on their final disposition.''

''Bueno. I might wish to enjoy the shy one some
more . . . But, no, better just shoot them as usual. It would
never do for the general public to hear gossip about my
personal habits, eh?''

"No, my Presidente. It is well known the Savior of Mexico is a saint."

The people who were worried about Captain Gringo being in the Mexican seaport of Progreso might have worried less had they known he was actually far to the south, in Limon, Costa Rica, and in danger of drowning or worse, depending on whether the tide came in or somebody flushed a toilet first. He knew the sun was shining, somewhere, but it was black as a banker's heart down here as he followed his sidekick, Gaston, through the sewers of Limon on his hands and knees. He couldn't see what he was getting all over his hands and knees, but it didn't smell like violets, and when Gaston stopped short at a fork in the dank darkness ahead the big Yank wound up with his face in the seat of the smaller Frenchman's soggy pants. He moved back a bit to growl, "Have you been eating beans again?"

Gaston protested. "Mais non, and I shall thank you to stop sniffing at my derrière, you species of sex-mad puppy-dog! If I was that kind of a boy I would have retired from the Legion with a much higher rank."

"Bullshit, you know damned well you deserted the Legion because you didn't like noise, and if you didn't just fart in my face, who did?"

Gaston sighed and said, "The ventilation down here does leave much to be desired, hein? I think this sewer to the right is the one we should follow, Dick."

Captain Gringo grimaced in the total darkness and asked, "You *think,* you old fart? Don't you *know?*"

"Mais non, I am a soldier of fortune, not a sewer inspector. But it stands to reason drainage from higher levels must indicate higher ground to the right, and the jail stands well back from the sea wall. Come, let us march on. We have to get there before La Siesta, non?''

Gaston started crawling again with Captain Gringo bringing up the rear, dragging their repeating rifles. The job really called for at least a machine gun, but despite Captain Gringo's reputation as an ace machine gunner, a knockaround guy could hardly be expected to check in and out of posadas or board streetcars packing a heavy machine gun. So the .44-40 Winchesters they'd picked up in the flea market on the fly would have to do, for now.

Gaston said, ''Regard, I see light ahead! We seem to be approaching the end of this thrice accursed hole in the ground at last!''

''Swell. How do you know it's the manhole in the prison courtyard? I'm completely turned around down here, and I know for a fact my sense of direction is better than yours, Gaston.''

''Merde alors, how many ways in and out of this maze could there be? Trust me, Dick. I told you I had it all mapped out in my head.''

They crawled on. Somewhere in the real world above some son of a bitch pulled a chain, and Captain Gringo caught the wet results in the small of his back. He cursed and Gaston laughed, saying, ''Regard the bright side, Dick. It could have been my ass, or your head, non?''

''Just keep moving, damn it. I'm right under the fucking pipe!''

Gaston did. A few minutes later they'd reached what looked very much like the bottom of a brick-lined well with leopard spots of sunlight gleaming on the flat floor of crud-covered cement and a rusty iron ladder running up to the manhole cover ten or twelve feet above their heads. No other tunnels pierced the circular wall around them. They were in a dead end. Captain Gringo leaned the two rifles against the slimy bricks and moved up the ladder. When he got to the top, with his bare blond head against the bottom of the rusty manhole cover, he could see out just a little.

The first thing he saw was a woman's bare snatch. A dame was standing smack on the cover in a loose campesina skirt and few peon women wore underpants. Okay, it was possible they allowed women inside the local lock-up. But how was he supposed to edge the rim up for a better look with her standing on the goddamn lid?

He tensed on the ladder rungs as a male voice suddenly called out, "Tengo cabanja por comerme un plato criollo, señorita!"

Then he relaxed some, as he realized the guard or whatever was only saying he was homesick for some old-fashioned Creole grub. But was that a sensible conversation to be holding in a prison yard?

It got even sillier when the dame standing on his head replied, "El pollo no esta cocinado todavia, señor." And Captain Gringo figured out what he'd been smelling besides shit lately. He swore softly, slid down the ladder, and asked Gaston, "Know any other neat shortcuts? We're under the *marketplace*, you chump! A mujer is selling home-fried chicken topside. Or she will be, any minute. She just told a guy her chicken wasn't done yet."

Gaston reached in his shirt pocket for a smoke as he sighed and said wistfully, "That reminds me, I have not eaten since the crack of dawn and it must be past my usual lunchtime."

"Don't light that!" Captain Gringo warned, explaining, "Aside from cigar smoke coming from a sewer grate striking people as a bit unusual, striking a match surrounded by sewer gas could be injurious to one's health. We're going to have to backtrack. There's no way they could be fixing to execute Sanchez in the public market, see?"

Gaston put the cigar away again, took out his pocket watch, and consulted it by such light as there was down here. Then he said, "I give up, Dick. Somewhere, back there in the maze, we made a wrong turn. There is simply no way we are going to make it, if they really mean to execute the boy against the courtyard wall before La Siesta!''

Captain Gringo said, ''You haul the guns. I'll take the lead this time. We've got at least ten minutes.''

He dropped to his hands and knees and started crawling back down the murky channel they'd come in by. Gaston naturally followed, but bitched, ''It's no use, Dick. We're never going to make it in time. Sanchez was a nice boy, I am sure. But he did get caught and they are going to shoot him, whether we crawl through another kilometer of this merde or not, hein? Slow down, damn it! You know as well as I you have no idea where you are going in such a hurry and as I told you, there are said to be salt-water crocodiles down here, closer to the waterfront!''

''Don't be silly. Would you crawl around down here in this shit if you had anywhere else to live?''

''Mais non, but I am not a meat-eating reptile, and some of the rats we have met this morning in passing look très yummy, even to me. Remind me never to start one of these très fatigué adventures of yours on an empty stomach again!''

Captain Gringo told him to shut up, adding that conversation, like cigar smoke, made people nervous, coming out of sewer vents. So they moved silently back to the Y-shaped junction Gaston had guessed wrong about. Gaston didn't comment until they'd backtracked even farther. Captain Gringo said, ''I figure that one tube has to lead downslope to the seaward outlets, too. But we passed a grated opening getting this far and the more I think about it, the surer I am we overshot the jailhouse by at least a couple of blocks. The main marketplace is south of the local lock-up, right?''

''Oui, and the map says a sewer pipe draining the courtyard leads into this main channel at a right angle. But—''

''But me no buts,'' cut in Captain Gringo, feeling in the pitch-black darkness with his free hand until his fingers scraped on a smoother, rusty wet surface and he added, "Yeah, here it is. Some asshole's stuck a steel plate over the old opening. We must have not been the first guys who ever thought about escaping from the prison yard via the storm drain. They must have put this here to keep *other* guys from trying it."

Gaston wedged up beside him, felt the boiler plating himself, and said, "Eh bien, that does it, then. Even if we had a cutting torch, and even if we were mad enough to light a cutting torch in a sewer filled with explosive methane gas, they are doubtless urging Sanchez to finish his last meal at this very moment, hein?"

Captain Gringo got out his pocket knife, unfolded the screw-driver blade, and started feeling for screw heads as he said, "Look, they put this plate here to keep guys in on the *other side*. But they have to have a way to open it once in a while from this side. The courtyard drainage can't *all* run through these holes punched in the plate. There must be some way to clean out the crud trapped on the far side and . . . Here we go, and the screw heads must be brass. They're not rusted in!"

Gaston said, "Eh bien, but it's still too late, Dick. Trust me on military executions; I have been on both sides of the firing squad, more than once. By now the courtyard above us will be filling up with the off-duty curious, anxious to have a good seat before the show begins. The original plan called for us to move in early, on the feet of the adorable pussy, and—"

"Shut up," snapped Captain Gringo, freeing a screw and starting on another as he growled, "The plan called for us to rescue Sanchez, period. We took the front money and we promised the guy's friends and family we'd do our best. Punking out at this late stage is hardly what I'd call the old college try, God damn it!"

"Oui, but we are soldiers of fortune, not football players, Dick. I enjoy heroics as much as the next idiot. Mais only within reason. You know that even if we could rescue Sanchez, this late in the final quarter, we would be giving up our live-and-let-live understanding with the only police force south of Texas that has, so far, let us live. Costa Rica is not going to like this, no matter how it turns out, and unless my watch is très fast, it promises to turn out très noisy!''

Captain Gringo got another screw loose and said, "You should have thought of that before you made the deal with those Costa Rican rebels, you money-hungry old bastard. It wasn't *my* idea to rescue Sanchez. I would have figured any asshole trying to overthrow one of the few halfway decent governments down here deserved what he was getting. But, no, you had to take the front money and introduce me to the guy's sad-eyed wife and kids, so here we are, and here we go, that was the last screw. Help me move this plate without sounding like a Chinese New Year's Eve.''

Two two soldiers of fortune manhandled the plate silently out of the way. As they did so, both gagged and Captain Gringo gasped, "Get a good lungful of what's out here and hold your breath the rest of the way! The tunnel ahead's filled with pure gas!''

"Merde alors, you call that *pure?*'' sighed Gaston as he covered his face with a kerchief to follow. Captain Gringo didn't answer. He couldn't. The badly drained sewer under the prison courtyard was a choking hell of odorless methane and hydrogen sulphide that smelled like rotten eggs. Both were explosive and both were poisonous to inhale. So he didn't inhale as he crawled like a lizard over hot rock until he reached the trap at the far end and could stand. As Gaston joined him, he took a cautious sniff and whispered, "The gas is heavier than air. It's okay to breathe above waist level, I hope, but don't overdo it!''

He took one of the Winchesters and started up the ladder toward the manhole cover above them. Thanks to the perforations in the cast-iron cover, they could hear what was going on topside, as well as see, sort of, what they might be up to.

They'd timed it close. As Captain Gringo reached the top of the ladder he could hear the corporal of the guard giving orders to present arms. There wasn't time to eavesdrop further. A firing squad presented arms just before it fired!

The big Yank took a deep breath of pure stink, gathered his powerful legs up under him, then levered a round in his Winchester's chamber as he braced his back and shoulders against the bottom of the manhole cover, and *heaved!*

The officer of the day, standing on the cover, was the first to sense something very unusual was going on as he was dumped on his ass, shouting, "Terremoto! Temblor de tierro!" in the mistaken conclusion it was an earthquake. Earthquakes were much more usual in Central America than the sight of what seemed to be a big blond jack-in-the-box, covered with crud, popping out of the ground with a repeating rifle in its hands, firing as fast as it could lever round after round in the chamber!

Captain Gringo mowed down the firing squad between him and the white-clad prisoner against the wall across the way and shouted, "Sanchez! This way! Poco tiempo!" before he turned on the ladder without waiting to see what Sanchez was doing. He turned just in time. The officer of the day was sitting up, pistol in hand, just in time to catch a .44-40 slug with his left eye socket. Captain Gringo potted a soldado in the distance who hadn't come unstuck yet. Then the magazine was empty and Sanchez, hands still tied behind him, was trying to dive headfirst down the manhole with Captain Gringo. The big Yank dropped the useless Winchester, caught the desperate young Costa Rican by the belt just in time, and lowered him head first to Gaston, who already had his own knife out to cut the boy's hands free, saying, "Eh bien. Follow me, tout de suite, and try not to breathe!"

Captain Gringo slid down the ladder to follow both of

them as he grabbed the Winchester that was still loaded.
Sanchez, of course, inhaled some sewer gas on the way to
the main sewer channel and passed out between them.
Captain Gringo abandoned the remaining rifle to haul the
unconscious youth along while, behind them, he heard
some dumb bastard yelling, "After them! They are trying
to escape by way of the sewers!"

By this time they were out of the gas-filled tunnel.
Captain Gringo growled, "What does he mean, *trying?*
Gaston, take the lead. Get us back under that marketplace
on the double!"

Gaston was already crawling fast, but called back, "Eh
bien, then what? Do you really think it wise to erupt like
some species of volcano in such a public place, Dick?"

"Keep going. We have to get out of this maze *some*
damned place and at least I know where we'll *be* if we
come up some place I've *been* before! Sooner or later
some wise ass is going to think about sending guys with
guns to cover all the ways out. So let's get out sooner.
Can't you move any *faster*, damn it?"

"In pitch blackness, on my hands and knees, in a maze
filled avec rats and crocodiles? But of course! Watch my
smoke! How is our passenger doing back there, Dick?"

"Not as well as he could if I could wake him up. The
fucking gas is following us and I don't feel so chipper right
now, either. So pick 'em up and lay 'em down before all
three of us pass out!"

Gaston did. They were soon in the dimly lit trap under
the market, and as Gaston leaned Sanchez against the
slimy bricks to slap him either silly or awake, Captain
Gringo eased up the ladder again to find the same dame
was still standing on the manhole behind her same chicken
stand. He sighed and reached in his pocket for a fistful of
change. Below him, the bewildered youth they'd rescued
opened his eyes to ask blearily, "Where am I, and who the
hell are you guys?"

Gaston said, "Later. Are you ready to move fast and do

just as we say if you ever wish to see your trés adorable little family again?''

Sanchez nodded weakly, and said, ''Sì, if I have to. I thought I was a goner, back there.''

Gaston said, ''You have to, and you were. Move up the ladder after our friend, the mooselike object above you, hein?''

As the Costa Rican started climbing, Gaston cocked his head, cursed, and quietly called up, ''Dick! They're in the tunnel behind us, coming fast!''

Captain Gringo muttered, ''I noticed. Sanchez?''

''Sì?''

''Stay right on my tail. Don't worry about where I'm running. I'm not sure myself, yet. All set?''

''Sì, I shall follow you through hell, amigo. It has to be an improvement on where I just *was!*''

Captain Gringo nodded, put the money in his mouth, then took out a match to hold between his lips like an unlit cigarette before he drew the .38 double action from his shoulder rig, braced himself, and heaved the manhole open.

The market woman standing on it weighed less than the officer of the day who'd last experienced such an event. So she flew farther, to land with her skirts up around her bare hips, screaming like a banshee as her chicken cart rolled the other way, scattering hot grease and fried chicken into the startled crowd while Captain Gringo and his two comrades popped out of the pavement at them!

Captain Gringo spat a mouthful of coins at the outraged woman to pay her for any damage he'd done her goods and dignity. Then he struck the big wooden match aflame and dropped it in the manhole they'd just climbed out of. The results were even noisier than he'd hoped for as the mixture of air, methane, and hydrogen sulphide blew manhole covers high in the air all over town.

It probably didn't do anyone down in the sewers at the moment a whole lot of good, either. But Captain Gringo wasn't about to hang around and watch. He was already running through the crowd, only knocking down those rude enough to stand in his way, as Sanchez and Gaston bulled after him through the total chaos. Gaston thought it only right to grab a wooden pole in passing, dumping shelves of produce and a big, flapping awning in their wake as somewhere a police whistle chirped plaintively for answers to all the confusing noises. Then Captain Gringo was running up the cathedral steps and into the incense-scented darkness beyond with his pals right behind him. As he ran down a side aisle toward an exit he remembered from a more sedate visit with a religious girlfriend, an old woman praying in one of the pews screamed maledictions after them. But an altar boy lighting candles as they passed merely shrugged, as if he was used to maniacs attending church between services.

Captain Gringo led the way out into and across a graveyard, paused behind a tomb near the far wall, and grabbed the still groggy Sanchez by the seat of his pants and the scruff of his shirt. He said, "Upsy daisy!" and heaved Sanchez over the wall. Gaston growled, "Please, Mother, I'd rather do it myself!" So the three of them were soon over the wall, and if Sanchez was acting dopey again, what the hell, he was easy to carry between them as they moved down the alley to a pateo gate Captain Gringo remembered well enough to kick open with his big mosquito-booted foot. They hauled Sanchez inside and spread him on the weeds. As Gaston shut the gate after them the bewildered Costa Rican sat up and gasped, "Jesus, Maria, y José! You guys sure move around like spit on a hot stove! Where are we now, and what if they call the police?"

Captain Gringo took out an Havana claro and struck another match to light it as he said, "They won't. This property is deserted. I know because just the other night I was screwing a local girl right where you're sitting. She was the one who told me the family that owned this property just moved up to the highlands. Nobody but a few of the local street kids know it yet. Let's make sure the cops don't. Come on, Sanchez. Are you escaping from prison or taking a fucking sun bath?''

Gaston helped him up as Captain Gringo moved to the back of the house to try the rear entrance. It was locked. No problem to a guy who'd put away his .38 to get out his knife again. The knockaround Yank picked the lock politely, to avoid needless damage, and led them inside. The house was a bit gloomy with all the windows shuttered and drop cloths draped over the remaining furniture that apparently would be sold with the house, when and if.

There was no food in the kitchen, unless one wanted to count a string of red peppers on one stucco wall. None of them were quite that hungry yet. Captain Gringo tried the sink pump. It worked. He grinned and said, ''Something had to go right today. Bueno. We can rinse our duds out in this sink, clean ourselves with rags as well, and walk out of here after La Siesta looking like proper little gentlemen after all. How far is your hideout from here, Sanchez?''

''In God's truth, I am not sure. Was that the main cathedral we just tore through back there?''

''Beats me. I don't know Limon that well. But it was named for the Fourteen Holy Martyrs, if that means anything.''

Sanchez brightened and said, ''I know where we are now. My wife and children are less than five blocks from here! I could make it in one dash, no?''

Captain Gringo shook his head and said, ''No. It's broad-ass daylight out, and the cops know we're somewhere in this part of town.''

''Bah, I spit in the milk of their stupid mothers! It is well known the police of our most corrupt and inefficient government could not catch the clap if it really wished for to get away from them!''

The two soldiers of fortune exchanged glances as Captain Gringo went on filling the kitchen sink. Gaston shrugged and said, "Oui, for this we just risked our lives and no doubt made the très inefficient police who just caught it mad at us as well! I told you you were a sentimental fool, Dick."

Captain Gringo grimaced and said, "What can I tell you. Everyone deserves a second chance." He turned to Sanchez and said, "Look, amigo, your political views are your own business. We just got paid to get you out of the mess you were in back there. So please don't get in any more before we can deliver you alive and pick up the bonus from your pals. Let's get out of these shitty duds. There's no soap, but a good squishy rinse ought to work most of the fresh crap out of the cloth."

Sanchez objected, "It will take hours for our clothes to dry, no?"

Captain Gringo growled, "Hours we got. La Siesta won't end until at least three P.M., and when La Policía see anyone out on the streets *during* La Siesta they always seem to want to know why."

"But I am so close to home! I have not seen my wife since they arrested me and—"

"So go jack off in a corner, you jerk-off!" Captain Gringo cut in, adding, "The game is staying alive. Not getting laid or even bouncing kiddies on one's knee, see? You got picked up in the first damned place because you went out to buy a present for your wife with every cop in Costa Rica looking for you after that bungled guerrilla raid. Now you want to run five blocks in broad-ass daylight, less than an hour after busting out of jail? You're right, the current government of Costa Rica must be inefficient, if you're a product of the local educational system!"

The big American finished stripping off his soiled duds and dumped everything but his boots, gun rig, and pocket contents in the tepid water as Gaston began to follow suit. Sanchez asked how they were to bathe themselves without wash rags, adding he saw none around.

Gaston said, "Every stick of furniture is covered with clean white cotton, merde alors! Can't we just shoot him, Dick? The idiot doesn't know how to wash his own balls and he wants to overthrow the government of a stable democracy! I do not know about you, but the company of lunatics makes me très nervous!"

Sanchez looked so worried Captain Gringo took pity on him, told him Gaston was just kidding, and moved into the next room, naked save for boots and gun, to gather some clean cloth for them all. He ripped a drop cloth in three good-sized hunks and was about to return to the kitchen with them when he heard something that froze him in place.

Unless a mouse was nibbling at metal for some reason, someone was trying to pick the same back door he'd just opened and relocked a few minutes ago. He eased to the kitchen door, hissed, "Company!" to Gaston as he tossed in the sheeting, then moved toward the nibbling sounds with his gun muzzle trained on the thick oaken door.

Whoever was trying to pick the lock this time didn't know what he or maybe she was doing. Captain Gringo waited on the far side until he got tired of waiting for them to either bust in or go away. Then he shrugged, grabbed the inside latch with his free hand, and swung the door open, to snap, "Congelos!"

The two girls on the back veranda froze as directed, staring wide eyed at the apparition of a big, blond, naked man pointing a gun at them. Then the one who knew him, in the Biblical sense, gasped, "Deek, what are *you* doing here?"

"Doing my laundry. Inside, both of you, poco tiempo!"

The muchacha he'd had in the grass out back a few nights ago—if only he could remember her fucking name as well as her fucking—nudged her better-looking friend, and the two of them did what any sensible people would with a gun trained on them; they stepped inside. Captain

Gringo slammed the door shut behind them and made sure
it was locked again before he lowered the muzzle of his
.38 to a more polite angle and said, "Okay, ah, Dulcenia?
My pals and I ducked in here to get cleaned up and sweat
out la siesta unobserved. Now it's your turn."

The pretty but rather hard-looking Dulcenia shrugged
and replied, "Like yourself, we wished for to get out of
the hot sun and perhaps have a little fun while the owners
of this old house are away. How did you get so steenky,
Deek? You smell as if you just crawled out of a cesspool!"

"Close enough. Aren't you going to introduce me to
your friend?"

She laughed and said, "Oh, this is Anita. I told her
about us."

Anita, who was maybe five years younger and not as
shop worn as the ready-for-anything Dulcenia, wasn't
staring at the naked American's face as she said, with a
Mona Lisa smile, "Sí, I thought she was just boasting
when she complained of internal injuries. Do you always
run around naked with your deadly weapons exposed,
señor?"

He grinned down at her and said, "Don't be scared.
Neither one is pointing at you right now." Then he turned
back to the older and tougher Dulcenia to ask in a more
serious tone, "Why were you two trying to break in and,
more important, who were you planning to meet here?"

"Deek, are you accusing me of being unfaithful to
you?"

"Why not? I don't recall us exchanging vows the other
night. It was you who told me about this property being
vacant when I picked you up at El Paseo. I'm not being
jealous. I just have to know if you girls planned to let
some other guys in once you made sure the coast was
clear, see?"

"Do you see any hombres with us, Deek? I told you,
we just wished for to, ah, look around."

"Yeah, I noticed a lot of the furnishings were still here. Okay, come on in the kitchen and meet the gang."

He didn't lead them, he herded them into the kitchen, where Sanchez still had his shitty pants on and Gaston was wearing nothing but his own .38 and a bemused smile.

Gaston had already wiped his old hide clean with a damp rag and tossed another to Captain Gringo as the somewhat awkward introductions were made. Captain Gringo wiped himself with the clammy cloth, at least where he needed to most, as Gaston questioned the girls in his own way about their sudden interest in real estate. He got about the same answers, smiled crookedly, and told Captain Gringo, "They don't look like lesbians to me. So it's burglary. Front door?"

Captain Gringo shrugged and said, "No way to get a wagon in through that narrow alley gate. Nothing left in the house one could cart off any other way. So, yeah, a bold-as-brass approach during La Siesta might work, should anyone bothering to look notice the front entrance opened from inside by someone who looks like a housemaid. Where did you get that black dress and apron, Dulcenia?"

"Oh, Deek, what are you accusing me of? I told you the last time we, ah, met that I worked in a cantina, remember?"

"Yeah, and you were wearing your cantina girl's flamenco skirt and off-the-shoulder campesina blouse from work, too. Gaston, did you ever have the feeling a lady was fibbing to you?"

"Oui, the first time I was fool enough to pay the rent in my très misspent youth. It was most annoying as well as difficult to understand when the virgin who said she'd run away from a convent gave me my first dose of clap."

Gaston took Dulcenia by the arm as he added, "We'll cover the back from upstairs. You two will naturally want to keep an eye out front, hein?"

Dulcenia protested, "Hey, I thought I was with Deek!" as the wiry little Frenchman led her out of the kitchen, whether she wanted to go with him or not. Captain Gringo

ignored Anita for the moment to tell Sanchez, "Find a
broom handle or something and give all those duds in the
sink a good churning. Put your own pants in, too, for
God's sake, and change the water a couple of times. We'll
be upstairs if you need us."

"Wait," protested Sanchez, "I have no weapon! What
if someone else tries to break in down here?"

"That's why Gaston and me are covering both entrances,
of course. Nobody's about to get in either way without a
battering ram and a steel skull. Meanwhile, the sooner you
rinse out those duds and spread them to dry, the sooner
we'll be able to see you home. So *do* it!"

"Where do I spread them to dry, on the grass out
back?"

"Jesus, haven't you ever hidden out before, Sanchez?
You spread 'em in front of that beehive fireplace in that
corner and light a charcoal fire, see?"

"Build a fire in this kitchen, as hot as it already is this
late in the day?"

"You're learning. Our linens will dry in no time and the
next-door neighbors won't wonder what they're doing in
the pateo of a house that's supposed to be empty. If it gets
too hot in here, go in the living room or, hell, come on
upstairs and join the fun."

Sanchez stared primly at the delicately blushing Anita
and said, "Señor, I am a married man."

Captain Gringo told him that was his problem and led
Anita out. As they headed for the stairs, she protested,
"Don't I have anything to say about this, ah, Deek? I
confess I am not a virgin who just escaped from a convent,
but, damn it, you might at least say somethimg romantico
to a girl before you rape her!"

He herded her up the stairs, saying, "The rape part is
optional. First we find a window overlooking the front
entrance. Then we see if I trust you enough to get
romantico, see?"

At the top of the stairs, he didn't try to find out where

Gaston and Dulcenia were. Old Gaston acted silly at times, but when he said he'd be guarding a post, nobody had to worry about it. He led Anita toward the front of the house, kicked open a door with his still booted foot, and sure enough it was a front bedroom.

Better yet, they'd left at least the bare mattress on the four-poster near the windows. The windows were french, though jalousied with slitted shutters from top to bottom. He cracked one open to see they led out onto a second-story balcony just large enough for a lady to stand on during a serenade, or to fire up and down the calle nicely from. He left the jalousies agape and told Anita to make herself comfortable as he hauled a heavy chest across the doorway to make it difficult for anyone to get in, or out, by surprise. When he turned around, gun in hand, he saw Anita had taken him at his word and was seated on the bed, removing her clothing.

Since she'd only arrived in a circle skirt, blouse, and sandals, there wasn't all that much to remove. She lay back across the bare mattress in nothing but her bare brown complexion to sigh, "I wish they had left the pillows, but then, a pillow under me with a man like you could ruin me in any case, no?"

The weapon she seemed most interested in twitched with sudden interest despite the fact it was supposed to take orders from his brain. But Captain Gringo was alive at the moment because the rest of him took orders from his more sensible organ. He said, "Hold the thought" as he sat down beside her to cover the front entrance through the slit in the french windows near the head of the bed. Anita sighed and said to the ceiling, "Just my luck. I finally meet a man who's hung right and he turns out to be some kind of a bird watcher. There is nothing out there, Deek. It is High Siesta and by now even the birds have gone home for to sleep, or at least for to have good fun in bed, no?"

He placed his free left hand in her fuzzy lap to comfort her as he said, "Sí, sí, un momento, querida. I hear a wagon coming along the calle. So somebody else must not know it's La Siesta out. I wonder who on earth it could be.''

Anita placed both palms against the back of his hand and spread her lush tawny thighs to be finger fucked as she purred, ''Who cares if some pobrecito is late getting home? Come home to Momma, querido!''

His old organ grinder must have thought it was a swell idea, from the way it was throbbing, fully erect, between his own bare thighs. But he put nothing but his free hand in old Anita's throbbing love box as he held the gun in the other and listened with some interest as the wagon stopped out front and, sure enough, someone started pounding on the front door downstairs.

''You want to tell me about it, now?'' he asked Anita, who just kept moving her hips in time with his finger strokes and moaned something dumb about wanting the real thing, now, por favor.

He said, ''Bullshit. You and your boyfriends planned to loot this house. So, look, that seems fair, doll. My own pals and I didn't bust in with engraved invitations from the owners and there can't be five hundred colones' worth of mighty heavy shit to carry off. I just want to know if those guys who came to strip the place are sensible guys or not, see?''

''I do not know what you are talking about! Oh, fuck me, por favor! I am almost there and I do not wish for to waste it on this kid stuff!''

Downstairs a gruff male voice called out, ''Hey, Dulcenia? Open up, damn it. Are you *in* there, Dulcenia?''

The girl he was fingering froze, despite the rather undignified position she was in, and stared up at Captain Gringo with fear-filled eyes. He chuckled softly and said, ''Perfidy, thy name is Woman.''

''On my mother's grave,'' she sobbed, ''it was not my idea. Kill Dulcenia. Don't kill me, querido! I love you too much for to ever betray you!''

"Never mind whose idea it was. Who the hell are those guys you two agreed to let in, and try the truth for a change, damn it!"

She started to cry as she replied, "It is Dulcenia's, you know, and my brother, Juan. They are not armed. They are only ladrones, not really malo, see?"

"Okay, just keep quiet and let's find out how serious they are about getting in. I'm not all that malo, myself. So don't shout any silly warnings to your brother and that pimp if you want to keep this a friendly occasion!"

He strained his ear as he heard the men down in the street muttering in consultation. Obviously, had they intended to just break in and to hell with public opinion they wouldn't have sent the girls around to the back, one of them disguised as a maid. So there was still some hope they'd just go away, figuring the girls hadn't been able to pick the lock out back, which was reasonable when one thought about how clumsy Dulcenia could be with a hat pin.

The matter was decided in a manner Captain Gringo wasn't expecting and wouldn't have chosen, had it been up to him. Another male voice called out, "Hey, you two with the wagon. For why are you trying for to get in this house, eh?"

The one who'd been yelling for the girls to open up replied in the voice of sweet reason, "Is this not numero cinco cinco, officer?" and the cop of course replied, "Pero no. It is uno dos dos. Cinco cinco is a good six blocks from here. What's up? For why are you searching for *either* address during *La Siesta*, eh?"

"We go where the boss tells us, and he is a slave driver who seems to think money is more important than our health, officer. He told us to pick up a sofa at this address. Or, that is, at cinco cinco, Calle de Rosas."

The cop laughed and said, "Madre de Dios, you muchachos *have* been out in the sun too long! This is not Calle de Rosas and even if it was you are half a dozen blocks too far north! This house is empty. We are keeping an eye on it for the owners. Who in God's name told you this was the place you were sent to, eh?''

"Damn," replied the cool burglar in mock dismay, "I *thought* that kid we asked for directions looked sneaky. But for why would a boy wish for to give false directions to honest working men who had done him no injury, eh?"

The cop sighed and replied, "When you have pounded a beat as long as me, you will know what a wicked world we live in, muchachos. Wise-ass kids are the least of my worries. The little shit must have thought he was being funny. The calle you want is three calles west, and the address is a good six blocks south. Go with God, if you must, or take the advice of a friend and get out of this hot sun until La Siesta ends, boss or no boss. That is what *I* mean to do, as soon as I finish this round. On a day like this, even the crooks won't be back on the streets until three, eh?"

Everyone out front laughed, and Captain Gringo allowed himself a modest chuckle as he heard the wagon drive off. He left the window agape but wedged the .38 between the mattress and the headboard as he told Anita, "All's well that ends well. Where were we before we were so rudely interrupted?"

But as he started stroking Anita's clit again she sobbed, "I wish for to go home! Let me up, por favor!"

He grinned down at her and said, "It's a little late to change your mind, kiddo. It was your idea to start this, for whatever reason. Now that you have my undivided interest . . ."

"No, wait. I do not wish for to be divided by your interest! You scare me. You have eyes of ice and . . . Madre de Dios, what is that big hot thing you are trying to . . . No! No! It is too big and I am no longer in the mood and you are *hurting* me, and *killing* me, and Jesusssss! Forget what I just said, querido mio!"

He did, as Anita locked her long, smooth limbs around

him to take everything he had to give her, to the roots, as she gritted her teeth, hissed in mingled discomfort and delight, then started moving in time with his thrusts, digging her nails in his bare buttocks as if to pull him deeper into her. He was willing. Aside from being a lot prettier than Dulcenia, whatever Dulcenia was doing at the moment, Anita was built smaller and nicer in every way. But knowing she was as tough a little street mutt as her tougher-looking pal, Captain Gringo didn't worry about treating her gentle, and she loved it when he treated her rough, to hear her tell it.

She sobbed, "Sí, sí, sí, pronto, pronto y profundo! Pound me deep and dirty, Deek!" So he did.

Even in the shaded bedroom it was getting hot and sticky as the tropic sun rose ever higher to bake the roof tiles of Limon. They were both soon slick with sweat as they rutted like pigs and, while he'd never thought of sex as dirty, he had to admit they were getting a bit gamey, for he'd just crawled through a sewer and Anita had apparently passed through a fish market in recent memory, judging by the way she smelled as he really warmed her up. But there was something to be said for honest human body odors, once one forgot one's drawing room manners. So he found hers sort of sexy, until, after they'd come twice together, old-fashioned, she asked him if he'd ever gone sixty-nine with a sweetheart. He had, of course, with ladies he'd admired more and shared a shower with first. But he told her Americanos didn't go in for such perverse Franco habits, and she told him he didn't know what he'd been missing. He said he was game for Greek loving, if she was, but Anita blanched and asked, "Do you think I am loco en la cabeza? I won't walk right for the rest of the week as it is! No woman could take that monster banana of yours up the ass and live! But let me up, I wish for to suck it, if only to have something to brag about when Dulcenia and I compare notes. She said you only screwed her in the grass out back three times, with all your clothes on. Es verdad?''

''I never kiss and tell. I don't eat pussy, either.''

She laughed lewdly, and shoved him off and over on his back to crouch above him, wiping his shaft with the hem of her skirt as she said, ''We shall see about that.''

He protested, ''Maybe another time, after we've both had a bath.'' But she didn't answer. She couldn't talk when her mouth was full. He closed his eyes and said, ''Jeeee-zussss!'' as her skilled, puckered lips slid up and down his reinspired shaft, tight and hot as the asshole she was probably lying about, too. He knew now he'd never in this world return the favor orally, now that he could see she'd had a lot of practice with oral sex, with a lot of guys he didn't know well enough to follow with his nose.

But what she was doing with her mouth seemed to excite her, and when she cocked a tawny thigh across his chest to present her gaping crotch for his full inspection, he was a good enough sport to put his hands up and play with her pinkness as skillfully as he knew how. And from the way she moaned in pleasure and started bobbing her head faster, he could tell he was doing something right. She seemed to enjoy having him hold her vaginal lips open with one hand as he slid two fingers of the other in and out while massaging her clit with his thumb. She began to bump and grind her pelvis above him and raised her head just long enough to hiss, ''Fantastico! Pero outrage my anus as well and put another finger in with the others, por favor!''

That sounded reasonable, and he found it sexually arousing as well to stare up into her vaginal opening as he played doctor, opening it up as far as it would stretch to abuse her internally with four, not three fingers in her love box while he ran the index finger of the other hand in and out of her rectum like a little dong.

She was treating him even nicer, with her amazingly tight lips and, Jesus, *tonsils?* So he gasped, ''We'd better switch back to the usual way if you don't want a mouthful of lunchar, doll!''

But she hissed, "Come in my mouth! Make me come, too! I am almost there, if only you would fill me more, querido!''

He was running out of fingers. But a gent always tried to oblige a lady. So he moved all four fingers deeper, till the knuckles of his left hand filled the pink rim of her vagina and then, what the hell, maybe the thumb would make it, if he was careful about the nail.

It did, just. Anita gasped but seemed to be trying to open wider as she felt what he was doing. So he shoved harder and suddenly his whole hand was in her to the wrist. She raised her head to bay at the ceiling, "Oh, glorioso! I have never felt so full! Do it! Do it! It must feel like this for to fuck a horse!''

He wondered if she'd ever tried that. There seemed to be no end to the deceptively innocent-looking Anita's sexual experimentation. But he found it oddly exciting to watch his wrist slide in and out of a woman like the shaft of a stallion as she madly sucked his own, while he sort of played Kitten on the Keys with his fingers inside her.

He came ahead of her, in her head. She didn't seem to notice as she kept on sucking, moving her hips in time with his fist fucking until she suddenly clamped down on his hand and almost cracked his knuckles in a long, shuddering orgasm. He shuddered too, and said, "Jesus, let's get back to normal before we kill each other.''

She didn't answer. She'd fainted.

He rolled her off, spread her thighs, and mounted her right to finish what she'd started, saying, "Damn, where did you go now that I really need you? Never suck a guy halfway off if you don't expect to finish, Sleeping Beauty!''

He came in her, fast, and lay weakly atop her, fighting to get his second wind, now that he could see she really wanted to fuck. Anita opened her eyes, smiled up radiantly, and said, "Oh, it's you. For a moment I thought I'd died and gone to heaven. Come to think of it, I have. My God, you make love fantastico, Deek!''

''You just noticed? You're not bad yourself, querida.''

''Do I fuck as good as Dulcenia?''

''Don't talk dirty. Why do you dames always ask the same dumb questions? Have I asked you who broke you in so swell, Anita?''

She giggled and said, ''You don't have to. You know no other man is as good as you at this! I thought Dulcenia was lying when she said you made her come three times without even any vice. I forget how far I am ahead of her, now. And wait until I tell her I took that monstrous thing in my mouth as well, eh?''

''What is this, some kind of a contest? What's the prize if you win, Anita?''

She started moving her hips under him teasingly as she replied demurely, ''This is the prize. Why have you stopped? Don't you like me anymore?''

He laughed and managed to move in her a little as he said, ''I like you a lot. But I'm only human. What say we stop for a smoke and if my spine ever comes back to life . . .''

''Don't stop yet! Please don't stop yet, Deek! I am too hot for to stop just yet.''

''So I notice. But, Jesus, we've been going at it hot and heavy for almost an hour and . . . Hmmm, come to think of it, my back does seem to be feeling better now.''

She raised her legs, locked her ankles around the nape of his neck, and reached down between them to start petting her own clit as she grinned up roguishly and said, ''Bueno, see if you can get it up my ass now, por favor.''

He frowned down at her and asked, ''Are you sure? You said, before. . . .''

''Never mind what I said before. I am trying to become a legend in my own time and Dulcenia only had you *one* way. I mean to pay her back for getting to you first, the bitch!''

He shrugged and said, "Well, as long as you girls are so fond of one another." But when he tried to get it in her anal opening, they could both feel it just wasn't meant to go in her that way. He said, "It's no use, Anita. You're just too tiny back there." But she said, "No, wait, maybe if I try for to fart, as you shove . . ."

He laughed despite himself and then, as he felt her rectal muscles dilating against the pressure of his glans, said, "Well, what do you know. I've never heard it expressed so delicately, but . . . Am I hurting you?"

"Si." she groaned, pulling him closer as she added, "But I love it! It feels so big this way, no?"

Actually he liked her front entrance as well, since his tastes were simple. But he knew maybe three out of ten dames got a perverse thrill out of sodomy, even if they had to strum their own banjo to come that way, and what the hell, cornholing a pretty girl had to beat cornholing a pretty boy. So he was cornholing her good when, out in the calle, somebody proceeded to shoot the hell out of something or somebody!

He stiffened, stiff in Anita's ass, as he counted at least a dozen gunshots in the distance and muttered, "What the hell?"

Anita pleaded, "Don't stop! Don't stop! I wish for to feel you shooting love up into my bowels, my great bull!"

That sounded fair. The gunfight, if it was a gunfight, had to be going on at least two blocks away and he, for one, had no intention of running out naked to get into it. But though he managed to satisfy Anita, and himself as well, once he'd come in her again he rolled off, wiped his rather brown shaft with the drapes near the head of the bed, and said, "No shit, we'd better get dressed and ready to run. That much gunplay is bound to attract attention and we don't exactly pay rent on this place!"

She grumbled but sat up and started to get dressed as Captain Gringo, still naked, clumped out in his boots to find out where Sanchez had spread their clothes to dry.

Sanchez hadn't. When he got down to the kitchen, Captain Gringo found his and Gaston's clothing still soaking in the sink and the beehive fireplace was still cold, or as cold as anything ever got in Limon. He called out, "Sanchez?" and got no answer. Gaston came in, wiping his own dong on a scrap of rag but otherwise armed. The little old Frenchman said, "I just heard shots. Where is that species of Sanchez?"

"Good question. Are you thinking what I'm thinking?"

"Oui, he said he was homesick. That was the direction he would have taken, too, the pin-headed species of asshole! Wait, I take that back, I've just been in an asshole and I feel sure it had more brains! How much time do you think we have, if there's enough of him left to talk?"

Captain Gringo hauled out Gaston's dripping pants and tossed them to him, saying, "Not long enough. Wring your duds out as best you can and let's vamoose!"

As they both twisted wet linen as dry as it would get, Gaston asked, "What about the girls?"

Somewhere in the house a door slammed and Captain Gringo grimaced and replied, "Yeah, what about 'em? It wouldn't have been smart to ask them to hide us, anyway. You know how stuffy Spanish-speaking guys can be when you fuck their womenfolk. Our hotel's out, too. The local law may have a good description of me, at least, and how many tall blond Anglos could be staying there? I'd say what we need about now is a three-island tramp steamer, going almost anywhere else!"

"Oui, but alas, this is not the banana-loading season. So the last time I looked, the harbor was almost empty." Gaston hauled on his wet pants, put on his wet shirt, and added with a shudder, "To think I was just complaining of the heat! How far do you think we can get, dripping and squishing, when everyone else in town is not only dry but indoors for La Siesta?"

Captain Gringo said, "I don't know. But we can't stay *here!*"

They both stiffened as out front someone started pounding on the door and a voice called out, "Policía! Open up!"

Captain Gringo added, "See what I mean?"

Captain Gringo struck a match in the fetid darkness, gulped when he found himself staring a human skull in the face, and said, "Forget what I said about the sewers you just dragged me through! Where do you come up with these neat shortcuts, Gaston?"

Gaston chuckled and replied, "It could be worse. The adorable dead in the drier catacombs around Mexico City tend to mummify avec somewhat grotesque expressions on their dried-out faces."

Captain Gringo held the match higher, illuminating other damp, mossy skulls grinning at them from the niches all around, and asked, "This is an improvement? Hey, what was that?"

"No doubt a rat," said Gaston, adding, "Otherwise, there should be nobody here but us chickens, hein? Come, let us make the tracks before those adorable cops find someone who might have seen us leaping gayly over the graveyard wall, hein?"

The match had burned down and had to be shaken out. But the crypt they were in seemed simply a long narrow tunnel leading south to who knew where. Captain Gringo followed as Gaston felt his way along the damp walls. Said walls were cut out of the bedrock under Limon, which was either very firm marl or awfully soft limestone and, worse yet, niched in a sort of elongated honeycomb pattern with the mortal remains of one or more human beings on every shelf. Some of them had been stuffed in sort of sloppy, or fallen into odd positions as they decomposed, so every once in a while a bone stuck out to try for a handshake in the dark. The smell wasn't so bad, considering. The catacomb smelled more like a mushroom cellar than what it was. Gaston had explained that the local custom was to bury people first in regular graves and then, as more space was needed in the modest churchyard, quietly dig up the bones and stack them like library books down here.

They'd made it out the back of the deserted house just as the Limon P.D. was battering in the front door. Fortunately the bush league cops had neglected to cover the back at first. But whistles had been blowing at both ends of the alley as they'd been trying to decide their next move, so their next move had been back over the wall of the cathedral burial grounds and then, since the front was exposed to view from the main avenue to the east, behind the biggest tomb they could find. It had been Gaston's idea to pick the lock of the bronze doors facing a wall some species of cop was bound to stick his adorable head over any minute.

They'd shoved their way into a spooky enough space no bigger than a peon's kitchen and manhandled some handy lead-sheathed coffins in place to barricade the door once they'd found they couldn't lock it from inside. Again it had been Gaston, feeling claustrophobic no doubt, who'd found the iron ring set in one of the stone slabs of the floor and decided it might be a meat idea to pull like hell and see what might be under it.

Captain Gringo had agreed, once they'd discovered at least one entrance to the catacombs that seemed to go with older Spanish-built cathedrals, that anything beat staying where they were until the cops got around to trying doors. So here they were, but where they were *going* was still up for grabs.

Gaston was sure the catacomb tunnel had to lead to the crypt under the cathedral, explaining, "It would never do to disturb the rest of the people in those expensive coffins we just left for the police to shove out of their way, hein? It makes more sense for the gravediggers to enter avec their grim loads via a more private entrance under the main building. The old Spanish were devoted to secret passages.''

Captain Gringo shrugged and said, ''Some guys collect stamps. Some guys dig secret passages. But what was the point of having that entrance in that family crypt back there?''

''One imagines it was an exit, rather than an entrance, Dick. In times of trouble, and there was a lot of that going on around here during the turmoil of the twenties, the priesthood may have considered the advantages of a hidden passage to safety should a sudden mob come to church shouting about Libertad and saying rude things about His Most Catholic Majesty's domesticated Spanish Church, hein? It never happened here in Costa Rica, the Costa Ricans being rather calm by nature next to some other Hispanics. But in Mexico some priests and worse yet, some nuns, were rather roughly handled in the first flush of democratic enthusiasm. Peasants who neither read nor write are a bit inclined to overdo Libertad. Ooops, end of the line! Some species of cochon has barred further progress with a door, locked from the other side, I fear!''

He started to strike a match. Captain Gringo said, ''Don't! I see a crack of light. Get out of the way. It looks as if lamplight from the far side is shining through between the door and the jamb.''

He traded places with Gaston and dropped to one knee to strain at the barely visible pencil line of dim light. He couldn't have seen it at all had not his eyes adjusted to the darkness by now. He got out his knife, saying, ''Yeah, there's a break in the light that has to mean the bolt. I'll just see if I can pry it up and... Damn, my pen knife is too short. Give me your snicker-snee.''

Gaston reached up to the damp nape of his shirt collar for the hidden hilt of the dagger few people knew he carried there until too late and produced the eight inches of cold steel, colder than ever after cooling all this time under a soggy shirt and jacket. Captain Gringo put his own knife away, took Gaston's, and slid the longer blade in the slot to see which way the bolt wanted to go. Somewhere in the darkness behind them something rumbled like distant thunder and Gaston muttered, "Hurry. Unless we're having a refreshing rain squall upstairs, the bastards have just broken into that tomb we were hoping they wouldn't!"

Captain Gringo neither hurried nor hesitated as he probed with Gaston's blade, found the bolt was a simple swing-up, and swung it up. Then he eased the door inward, peered out through the slit, and saw nothing more interesting than a candle sconce illuminating the cavernous arched crypt beyond. He whispered, "Let's go. Keep it down to a roar."

They naturally rebarred the door behind them and played peek-a-boo between the massive Romanesque pillars holding the floor of the cathedral above them up until they found a stone spiral stairway leading to a higher level. They eased up and peeked through the velvet curtains at the top. Captain Gringo said, "Shit, we're right near the altar crossing, and it looks like a mass is about to begin!"

Gaston said, "Eh bien, the mass can't last more than an hour or so and nobody should wish to visit the crypt during services, so why don't we just sit tight and . . . Forget what I just said. Someone is pounding on that door down there! Try to look inconspicuous as we stroll up the side aisle for the main entrance, hein?"

Captain Gringo didn't know what else to do. So he took a deep breath, stepped through the curtains with Gaston trailing, and nodded pleasantly to the little old nun he almost bumped noses with. She looked somewhat startled, but merely nodded in return as the two soldiers of fortune moved along the aisle, trying to keep the pillars between them and the robed churchmen doing something around the altar as other people filed in to take seats in the nave. Nobody seemed to be curious about them, but Captain Gringo felt as if he had at least a hundred-watt Edison bulb stuck in each ear as he walked primly as he knew how for what felt like a hundred miles.

Just as they'd almost made it to the open front door, lightning flashed outside and a mess of people dashed in, laughing or cursing depending on their natures, as it proceeded to rain cats and dogs outside. The last ones in were pretty soaked. Then the doorway was clear and they were about to step out into the rain. Only they didn't. Because a mess of cops were coming up the steps, guns drawn, as wet as well as mad looking as wet hens!

The two soldiers of fortune ducked back inside. Gaston said, "Take a pew. Take any pew." But Captain Gringo had already figured that was their only chance, so he got to the first empty seat. The two soldiers of fortune were sitting with the other worshippers, heads bowed, as the police tore in.

It didn't work. One of the cops spotted Captain Gringo's blond hair and Anglo Saxon features, muttered to his sergeant, then drew a bead on the two soldiers of fortune with his gun as the sergeant snapped, "You there, with the blond hair. Come out here and let us have a better look at you, eh?"

They hadn't mentioned Gaston. So the little semi-invisible Frenchman muttered, "Try to bluff. I'll cover you." But Captain Gringo had already figured that out as well; he was rising with a blank, innocent expression on his face. The police sergeant said, "Sí, usted. Over here, poco tiempo."

Captain Gringo pasted a smile across his numb lips and moved out to the aisle. The police sergeant was grinning, too, wolfishly, and he had more men with him than Captain Gringo had bullets in his hidden .38.

But then the same little old nun came flustering out of nowhere to demand of the police sergeant, "What is the meaning of this, young man? How dare you enter the house of God with drawn guns? Can't you see the mass is about to begin?"

The sergeant touched the bill of his cap respectfully and said, "Forgive us, sister. We mean no disrespect to you or God. We are in hot pursuit of two men who were just seen entering church property and this big foreigner answers the description of one of them!"

The nun stared thoughtfully at Captain Gringo, who was beginning to feel like a bug on a pin, then she asked the sergeant, "Did the men you seek come in through that front entrance?"

"Pero no, sister. We think they came in by way of the catacomb tunnel from the graveyard. We found a tomb that had been trifled with, judging from the fresh scratches on the bronze. The tunnels below are empty, but if they came up through the crypt—"

"They would have had to pass by *me*," the old nun cut in, adding, "That is where I am usually stationed, during mass, by the votive candles to the dead, near the doorway to the crypt. I only came from there, just now, when I saw how rude you and your men were behaving! Shame on you wicked boys! Are you Protestants?"

The sergeant grinned sheepishly and replied, "Pero no! But this one looks like an Anglo who *could* be, no?"

The old nun stamped a tiny foot on the stone floor and said, "If you are not Protestants you are idiots. Can't you see this young man is soaking wet?"

"His clothes do seem damp, but what of it, sister?"

"What of it, and you call yourselves *police* officers? It just started raining, no?"

"Sí, but . . ."

"Use the heads God gave you!" she cut in, touching Captain Gringo's damp sleeve to continue, "The poor boy is soaking wet, but as a better Catholic than you he dashed across the plaza for to attend mass anyway. The men you are searching for, whoever they are, would have been in the tunnels or who knows where when the storm broke only moments ago, no?"

The sergeant frowned at Captain Gringo, caught on, and

said, "Sí, forgive me, señor. I was not thinking. But you do look a lot like someone else we are searching for." Then he turned to his men and said, "Vamanos, muchachos. If they did not duck in *here,* they must be somewhere *else* in the neighborhood. Let us fan out and proceed to knock on doors, eh?"

Captain Gringo waited, standing by the tiny old nun, until they'd gone back out into the rain. Then he nodded soberly down at the nun and said, "Thank you, sister. That was very kind of you, but why?"

She said, "I don't know what you are talking about. It is my duty to see good Christians are not disturbed during mass and I know you are a good Christian, for I heard it from a priest. Go back to your pew and behave yourself until the mass is over, señor."

But as he turned away to do just as she said, she couldn't help giving a sweet little giggle and adding, "I can't wait to tell Mother Superior I just made Captain Gringo attend at least one mass for the good of his soul!"

Considering that the old priest conducting the post-siesta mass was considered a bit long-winded even by his admirers, and considering he was being considerate enough to drag the services out until the tropic squall let up outside, that was one short mass to Captain Gringo and Gaston!

As the cathedral began to empty, they still faced at least an hour and a half of late afternoon sunlight with nowhere to go and a lot of people mad at them by this time.

They already knew the local law was looking for them. By now the two whores, or, rather, their pimps, would be searching for them, either for revenge or to collect the rewards on them. For whether the girls had told them all the intimate details or not, both Dulcenia and old Anita had to be smart enough to figure they were wanted, seriously, by the authorities. And in Latin America, there was always at least a modest reward for turning outlaws in.

It got worse. When they stopped at a newsstand to pick up some extra smokes for what had to be a long night ahead, the Prenza de Limon blared headlines at them regarding the shoot-out earlier that afternoon and, yes, the cops had "recaptured" Sanchez by filling him with lead. Sixty-two bullets, according to the paper. Sanchez had no doubt stopped counting after the first couple of rounds in the head.

So there went the outside chance the jerk-off had made it safely home to the wife and kids and there went any chance to collect the final payment from his rebel friends. In fact, there went any chance to ever go near that part of town again. Latin rebels, like most kinds of people who spent lots of time plotting in dark cellars, tended to harbor macabre Machiavellian notions. So by now *they'd* be hunting for the soldiers of fortune who'd "double-crossed poor Sanchez" too!

As they sat under the awning of a sidewalk cantina to consider their options, it was Gaston, of course, who considered the *practique* option of simply turning police informers, explaining, "We are not wanted here in Costa Rica for anything else. If we told the police we were forced to help them spring Sanchez, and gave them the current address of his fellow rebels, with the understanding we would only mention possible rewards if we were forced to appear in court—"

"Forget it," Captain Gringo cut in, adding, "Two reasons. Aside from it being a shitty way to treat people who gave us half the money up front, guys in our line of work have their reputations to consider. Who in the hell would ever hire soldiers of fortune again if word got around they were Mike Finks?"

"True, but since the rebels are sure to spread the word in any case, why should we have the name without the game, hein? As you have often said in your droll Yankee way, Dick, one must eat one's apple a bite at a time, and the matter before the house, at this time, is to stay alive for at least a few more hours, hein?''

Captain Gringo sipped at his gin and tonic, then said, ''There are always cool heads as well as hot heads in any gang. By now they're expecting us to rat on them. So they'll have moved their secret headquarters, but they'll also be keeping an eye on it, if only to ambush the police raiding party. When nobody raids them, they may figure out what went wrong. It only took us a few hours to see. Sanchez was an impulsive asshole. They have to have known him better. But I like the suggestion about staying alive for at least a few more hours. Don't you know any other, ah, rogues, as you call them, here in Limon?''

Gaston considered, then shrugged and said, ''One. It is the long shot of long shots, but perhaps not as suicidal as trying to catch a train for San José with the adorable police clustered like grapes around the depot by now.''

''Okay, who are we talking about, damn it? We have to get off the goddamn streets before one of the many bastards looking for us by now gets lucky!''

Gaston sighed and said, ''I refer to one Abdul El Gemal, who claims to be from Spanish Morocco, mais I doubt it. The Bedouins we fought in North Africa in my salad days were fiends from hell, but even fiends have *some* standards. One could accuse Abdul El Gemal of regularly committing incest with a camel if one didn't know for a fact his mother died of the pox some years ago. He is what may be described as a labor contractor, hein?''

''Our kind of labor?''

''Mais non, I consider myself a soldier of fortune, not an outright bandit. But if anyone in Central America is planning to rob a bank or perhaps assassinate a popular archbishop, Abdul is the man to see about it. The only thing one may say in the bastard's favor is that, so far, he has never turned anyone in to the law for money. I imagine people in the market for professional killers pay better, hein?''

Captain Gringo grimaced and said, ''Well, anything's better than the frying pan we're in. So which way is the fire?''

''Down the waterfront a short but possible fatal hop. The slimy species of North African does his real business behind the front of très quaint Arabesque clip joint serving strong black coffee and weak-willed women, both at outrageous prices. But before I lead you down the primrose path, Dick, let us understand you may not like the set-up. I am less fastidious than you by far, and I have never wanted to work for Abdul El Gemal. Oh, by the way, did I fail to mention he was a flaming homosexual as well as a murderous bucket of slime?''

A couple of cops were sauntering up the street behind Gaston. So Captain Gringo placed some coins sedately on the tin table and said, ''Let's go. Anywhere has to be better than here, right now!''

They got up, swung the nearest corner without incident, and moved east to the waterfront quay to stroll innocently down it, staring wistfully at the few steamers anchored out in the Limon roads. Gaston said he didn't know the pursers on any of them.

Gemal's Seaside Attraction was one of those hole-in-the-wall joints that didn't advertise with a sign out front. You were supposed to *know* where it was. Gaston had just pointed out a dull red door beyond a chandler's shop when the door flew open and a sailor flew out head first to land face down on the cobblestones. Someone threw his hat out after him and slammed the door shut again with a high-pitched curse. Gaston chuckled and said, ''That was Boca the Bouncer. Boca must be in a good mood this evening. Our friend on the ground does not seem to be bleeding anywhere, hein?''

As the drunk crawled away on hands and knees Captain Gringo asked, ''Is this Boca a pansy, too?'' and Gaston replied with a shrug, "That would be hard to say. It wears a dress. But nobody has ever tried to look under it. I told you Abdul admires tough people."

Gaston shoved the door open and Captain Gringo followed him into another dark murk that smelled funny. They worked their way along the stucco wall, but none of the dark figures seated at the little tables would have recognized their own mothers in the lousy light had they turned to look. It was hard enough to see the belly dancer wiggling and jiggling under a coal oil lamp in the center of the floor, clad mostly in swirling cigar smoke. But she wasn't bad, if a man admired a little meat on his women.

Gaston was making for an archway screened with a beaded curtain when an even more curvaceous creature as tall as Captain Gringo barred the way and started to say something nasty before she, he, or it recognized Gaston and said, "Oh, it's you. Who's your handsome friend, Gaston?"

Gaston introduced them and added they had more important things to discuss with Abdul El Gemal. Boca the Bouncer goosed Captain Gringo in passing and told him not to go to strangers the next time he had a hard-on. The invitation might have seemed more inviting or more revolting if he'd been able to get a better look at Boca's face. As they went through the beaded curtain, he muttered to his guide, "You told me this place was rough, but you still might have warned me. Don't you know whether that big ape back there is male or female? Whatever it is, it seems to like me more than I like it!"

Gaston said, "Boca the Bouncer has a certain reputation for uncouth behavior to maintain. Do not worry about her, and I use the term out of common courtesy. Watch the cochon you are about to meet. If *he* says he finds your ass adorable, he *means* it!"

Gaston knocked on an oaken door solid enough for a bank vault and a prissy little Negro, stark naked and hence obviously a male—sort of—opened it a crack, recognized

Gaston, and called over his skinny black shoulder in lisping Arabic. Abdul must have wanted to see them after all, for the mariposa let them in.

Abdul El Gemal was sprawled on a pile of silk pillows in a niche across the expensively carpeted room. He was obscenely fat, oily, bearded, and dressed in too-tight red silk pajamas. He was smoking a burbling Mid-Eastern hookah. It didn't smell as if he'd charged his bubble pipe with tobacco. But for a man inhaling hashish the voluptuous North African seemed alert enough to follow the gist as Gaston gave him a hasty rundown on their recent troubles. When the little Frenchman had finished, the fat Arab nodded sagely and said, "Though Allah be more merciful, you two seem to be in a hell of a mess. But through the compassion of the One True God, you have come to the right place. Sit down. I have a proposition for you."

There wasn't a stick of furniture in the place. But as the two soldiers of fortune sat on the floor they found it soft enough. There had to be at least a dozen layers of Oriental rug under them.

Abdul snapped his fingers, and his black servant, slave, lover, or whatever crawled over to him to calmly open the fly of the red silk pajamas, haul out the large albeit limp dong of Abdul Gemal, and crouch naked between the Arab's fat legs to start sucking, with his skinny bare black rump presented to the visiting soldiers of fortune.

Captain Gringo grimaced and asked, "Does he have to do that right now? I thought you wanted to talk business, Gemal."

The labor contractor they'd come to see leaned back more comfortably and replied calmly, "Never pass up a chance to take a piss or enjoy an orgasm, my young friend. Some people can discuss business as they enjoy a luncheon together. I prefer my *own* creature comforts and I assure you I can add up the compound interest on a loan even smoking hashish, as I'm being, ah, smoked. Would either of you care to fuck this pretty youth as he blows me? As you can see, his ass is not occupied at the moment and I can assure you he's as tight as a schoolboy back there.''

Gaston nudged Captain Gringo to silence him as he told the degenerate flatly, "We would like to hear your more *sensible* business proposition, hein?''

Abdul took a deep drag of hashish, told the black boy to watch those fucking teeth, and said, "As you know, the Cuba Libre Movement has been trying to chase the Spanish out of Cuba since way back in '68. The Spanish have been holding on by making false promises, killing people who pester them about keeping them, and in general hanging on to their last profitable colony in Latin America with the old iron fist in a rather threadbare velvet glove.''

Gaston grimaced and said, "Merde alors, if you are talking about us signing up with the Cuba Libre dreamers, forget it! I don't know what is wrong with Cubans. Most of the Cubans I've met seem reasonable enough. But as *rebels* they simply do not have what it takes. You are most correct in saying they have been engaged in an off-again-on-again revolution of comic opera proportions for nearly twenty years. Everyone else down here seems to have had no trouble freeing themselves of the Spanish yoke with one sweet and short revolution. Obviously the Spanish Empire lacks the hair on its chest for a real free-for-all fight with serious men of action. So obviously the Cuba Libre types must be lazy idiots as well, hein?''

Gemal moved his fat hips sensuously in time with the mariposa's bobbing head as he replied calmly, "What you say is true. The Cuban rebels are more prone to make speeches than war, and every time they win a skirmish they allow the Spanish to ask for a truce and more pointless negotiations. But of late the situation has been changing for the better. Better, that is, for the rebel side. For one thing, after considerable back-stabbing and fighting among themselves, the Cuba Libre Party has at last agreed to a sensible leader. Tomas Estrada Palma has set up a government in exile in New York and while he still spouts the idealistic propaganda of the rebel poet, Jose Marti, nobody is following Marti's grotesque battle plans this season. Palma is a hard-headed realist, with the sort of man-to-man manner that appeals to North Americans. So he has the backing of more than one Gringo congressman as well as the Hearst newspaper chain, eh?''

Captain Gringo nodded. He still read the papers from back home, when he could get them, but said, ''We're not about to go to New York. Personal reasons.''

Abdul El Gemal moaned softly, and told his lover, ''That's enough for now, unless one of these other gentlemen would like to be sucked off.'' Then, when he noted the looks on his visitors' faces, he chuckled fondly and added, ''Go. I shall send for you the next time I am in the mood.''

As his love-slave simpered out, Gemal told Captain Gringo, ''If I had not heard of your troubles with the U.S. Army you would not be useful to me, either, Captain Gringo. Palma needs no office help in New York. He needs fighting men, real fighting men, for the all-out liberation of his homeland. A few of the usual machete swingers have risen as usual in the wilder eastern end of Cuba. The Spanish have a better than usual military governor in the form of Butcher Weyler. So the untrained and poorly armed guerrillas under Garcia are already in trouble. But if a serious force of professional soldiers, armed with the latest weapons—including the new machine gun—were to establish a beachhead near the Bay of Pigs, cutting Weyler's army in the field off from Havana—''

''It won't work,'' Captain Gringo cut in flatly, going on to explain, ''To land a force of any size you'd need a mess of boats, and Spain has a navy, ironclad, armed with big guns that go *boomp* in the night.''

Gemal yawned and said, ''Yes and no. Spain not only

has a fleet of ironclads, it also has a government one would not entrust with the task of rounding up stray dogs. The underachievers of the Spanish king's Cortes have been trying to save money because His Most Catholic Majesty spends it faster than even a brutal tax system can gather it. They dare not ask the Spanish nobility to cut down on personal luxuries. So they economize where they can, and they have not bought coal for the steam boilers of the Spanish navy in years. All those big tin boats are so much puffery. On the rare occasions they have to carry out some port ceremony they are forced to burn the local furniture.''

Captain Gringo shrugged and said, ''Maybe. Meanwhile, in my time, I've ducked more than one gunboat flying the Spanish colors. But even if we accept a Spanish navy mostly stuck in port, a landing force on the Cuban coast would still have its *own* seaborne logistics to worry about. Machine guns are swell, but they burn up six hundred rounds a minute. The guys in the landing force would probably want to eat once in a while, too. So no matter how much shit they carry ashore with them—and few men can lug more than sixty pounds anywhere important—what happens after the Spaniards notice the beachhead and start shooting back? Weyler's guys have to have at least one coast artillery piece to make any thin-skinned vessels coming in with more supplies feel sort of unwelcome, right?''

Gemal shrugged and said, ''I am a labor contractor, not a general. I'm sure the Cuba Libre officers who'll be leading you have some idea of provisioning you once you land. After all, they'll be *with* you, and not even a Cuban can live by cigars alone. Perhaps they mean to live off the country as your lines advance, eh?''

The two soldiers of fortune exchanged sober glances. Gaston said, ''Merde alors, live off a country in the wake of a retreating Spanish army? They would be free to loot more freely than any liberating force who ever meant to rule over a contented populace and, aside from idealism, there is the practique fact that most of the large estates away from the few Cuban towns grow nothing but cash crops of sugar and tobacco, neither of which is as filling to an army marching on its stomach as one might desire.''

Captain Gringo added, ''Screw the food. I'm still talking about *ordinance*. A guerrilla action is one thing. A no-bullshit war between even small armies calls for a steady supply of ammo. I can see where Butcher Weyler's army will get theirs. They'll be fighting in front of supply lines leading back to their own ammo dumps. We'd be forced to rely on friendly fishes, once shore fire drives our thin-skinned landing craft out of range. So haven't you got a more sensible job lined up for us, like wrestling alligators or tasting food for a tyrant?''

Gemal sighed and said, ''As Allah is the judge of my no-doubt doomed soul, none of my other clients are in the market for men of action at the moment. I could fix you up with a job as the bodyguard-lover of a certain dictator, if you'd like to demonstrate how well you can suck. Otherwise, I can only send you on to Progreso, or ask you to leave. I am not in the business of harboring fugitives from the local police, unless I have some *use* for them, and you lads say you have a rebel gang looking for you as well?''

''Tell us about Progreso,'' said Captain Gringo.

Gemal said, ''Progreso is a seaport on the coast of Yucatan. The Cuba Libre Party has made certain arrangements with the local Mexican authorities and what Mexico City does not know can't hurt anyone, eh? Contractors like myself have been sending all the soldiers of fortune we can recruit to Progreso. At the moment they still lack the numbers there to do much more than smell the pretty women and fuck the pretty flowers Yucatan is noted for. Once enough of you old pros are there, it shall be Palma's problem, not mine, to ferry you all to the Bay of Pigs on the south coast of Cuba.''

"How do you intend to get us to Progreso?"

"By banana boat, of course. I employ people who can draw passable paper money, free-hand, with a crow-quill pen. So you will board as supercargo agents of a nonexistent banana company and simply get off at Progreso when the steamer puts in there for fresh water, whether it needs any or not."

He yawned again, stretched, and added, "The steamer will not put in here until the morning tide, and of course my forger will need time to prepare your new identification papers. Do you have any names in particular in mind?"

Captain Gringo smiled thinly and said, "Surprise us. Guys making up names for themselves tend to screw up and grab a name out of thin air the cops might have on file as a known associate."

The oily Arab nodded sagely, clapped his pudgy palms, and said, "They told me you were intelligent as well as somewhat muscular. I seem to be falling asleep right now for some reason. My servants will see you to your quarters and if you desire anything, do not hesitate to ask. But don't hang about in the main room downstairs. The police drop by every once in a while to make sure my entertainers are not screwing the customers on the tables, uninvited."

A sultry-looking girl came in in response to Gemal's clammy claps. Gemal said something to her in Arabic, and she told them in Spanish to follow her. It didn't cause Captain Gringo any pain. She was built like an hour glass and dressed in what looked like pajama pants made of cobwebbing. She'd worn nothing at all above the waist but he sort of forgot just what her tits had looked like as he watched her nicely shaped behind jiggle under the thin gauze. He wondered idly why a woman's behind you could *almost* see looked yummier than totally nude tail.

She led them up a flight of stairs to a dimly lit hallway reeking of hashish and frankincense. There was a little myrrh burning somewhere, too. But somehow Captain

Gringo doubted she was leading them to the Manger, and he was right. She dropped Gaston off by one door and told Captain Gringo, "Just walk this way a little farther, señor."

He'd have felt silly walking that way any distance at all. She seemed to move her hips at least a foot sideways for every six inches forward. She led him through another doorway into a pitch-black room, struck a match to light a lamp left over from that story about Aladdin, and asked him how he liked it so far.

He stared around at an interior lifted from the same Arabian fairy tales as the lamp as he tried to figure out how the furniture worked. The floor and walls were covered with lush oriental carpeting. There was a low rosewood table with a bottle and a tray of candied fruit by a big pile of loose silk pillows that had to be the only seating, the only bedding, or both. He said, "I've always wanted to spend a night in a harem. Didn't expect it to be quite this, ah, empty, thought."

She got it. She smiled softly and asked, "Would you prefer a boy, a girl, or perhaps both to serve you, effendi, I mean señor?"

He laughed and said, "Hell, I'm just an old-fashioned boy. Two or three beautiful dames would probably do it for me."

He'd been half-kidding. But she told him to just have a seat and she'd serve his order in a minute. She added, rather coyly, considering, "I am called Fatima, if you do not find me too old and fat."

"How old and fat are you, Fatima?"

"Alas, though Allah be more merciful, I am almost twenty and few men desire me these days."

He laughed incredulously and said, "You must meet few real men on this job, then. I think you're pretty neat, Fatima. Why don't we lie down and talk about it?"

But she darted outside, sobbing something about what a nice guy he was. So he shrugged, moved over to the pile of pillows, and took off his jacket to sit down cross-legged. He tried a candied date. It was too cloying. He took a sip from the bottle. It wasn't bad, if only he could figure out what in the hell it was. It tasted of anise, allspice, and something that needed to wash under its arms more. But it was at least as strong as wine, so what the hell.

He lit a claro as he wondered how one got some cross ventilation in here. The room was a bit warm as well as overperfumed. He put his gun rig between the pillows and the wall and took off his shirt to see if he was sweating. He was. He wondered where the hell Fatima had gone, if she was coming back, and if she knew where the windows were hiding under all this Persian ruggery.

Fatima did come back, stark naked now, as were the two younger girls who followed her in, giggling. One was sort of shy looking as well as darker than even Fatima and almost boyishly slender. The other was more roundly built than Fatima and stared boldly at him, as if she wondered if he was man enough. He sort of wondered, too. She, alone, looked like a man-eater. She was pale skinned and had reddish hair, all over. He'd heard there were red-headed Bedouin tribes left over from the Vandal Empire of North Africa, unless, of course, she was descended from some Irish lady the Barbary pirates had picked up in their travels. Fatima said her name, or nickname, was Zigazig. The little shy one answered to Sharah. She was the one who dropped to her knees on the carpet in front of him and proceeded to haul off his boots as the red-haired Zigazig got between him and the wall to start trying to stuff him with candied dates. He told her no thanks, and when it was obvious her understanding of anything but Arabic was limited, asked Fatima to tell her to knock it off.

Fatima did so, sinking down beside him across from Zigazig to blush demurely and ask, "Would you like to get right down to sex? Who do you wish to do what to, first?"

He gulped and said, "Hold on, girls, you're going a little fast for me. I must be nuts. This is the daydream every man has at least once a day, but now that it seems to be coming true..."

Fatima nodded understandingly and said, "I'd better take charge."

Then she did, muttering in Arabic to her nude companions as she wrapped her arms around Captain Gringo, pressed her naked breasts against his bare chest, and shoved him over backwards under her as someone else proceeded to pull his pants down.

Sharah gasped and Zigazig clapped her hands in approval as they both saw what they were getting into, or what was getting into them. For despite his feelings of awkwardness Captain Gringo was naturally starting to rise to the occasion. Fatima asked if he minded being kissed on the mouth, which seemed an odd question, considering, and when he told her to be his guest, she was all over him, kissing like one of those new patent vacuum cleaners, only better. He'd never heard of a vacuum cleaner that tongued so skillfully. He wrapped his arms around her and proceeded to return the compliments with enthusiasm, now that the ice had been broken. He knew she expected to be laid first, and that seemed only fair. But then someone was sucking hell out of what he'd been about to put in Fatima, and since she was kissing his lips it couldn't be her, but what the hell, it sure felt great. For the lips working on his more private parts were skilled as hell, too!

He and Fatima came up for air in each other's arms. She said, "Oh, you kiss so nice. Do you like what we are doing?"

He said, "I sure do. But, uh, let's see, yeah, Zigazig, seems to be sucking me off while I'm kissing you! Is that what she's *supposed* to be doing?"

"Of course. I told her to. I thought you might enjoy

romantic foreplay, darling. Do you mind if I call you darling? I am feeling most romantic, too!"

"I noticed. This sure beats *working* at it, Fatima. But what are *you,* ah, getting out of it?"

She giggled and snuggled closer to chew softly on his collar bone as she rubbed against him sensuously. He looked down, saw the part in Sharah's black hair between Fatima's open thighs and said, "Right, silly question." Then Fatima was kissing him on the mouth with shuddering passion as she moved his free hand to play with one of her naked nipples. So he couldn't say anything more as they made hot Arabesque love, if that was what one called this weird business.

He had nothing to complain about as he lay across the pillows making lazy love to a beautiful woman while another one did all the work for him as Sharah, in turn, drove Fatima up the wall to a long shuddering orgasm in his arms. He ejaculated almost at the same time in one woman's hot wet skill while making love to another. But then he said, "Okay, enough of this foreplay, Fatima. I told you I was an old-fashioned boy!"

"You still want *me?*" She gasped with delight as he rolled her on her back and mounted her properly. He growled, "What do you mean, still? I haven't *had* you yet, doll!"

And then he did. Fatima hissed in pleased surprise as he entered her for the first time, despite all the slap and tickle they'd just gone through together. Fatima hadn't gotten a look at his shaft as her fellow love-slave or whatever, Zigazig, had nearly swallowed it alive. So Fatima made very complimentary remarks indeed as Captain Gringo, fully aroused by the weirdly nice surroundings, proceeded to screw her silly.

Fatima made love that way as well as any other and, in truth, she would have been enough for a guy stuck overnight with nothing to read in bed. But as he humped Fatima on the pile of pillows he was curious enough to

turn his head to see what Sharah and Zigazig had to say
about all this. He saw they were screwing, too. It was hard
to see how, since he was sure they were both girls. But the
wiry little Sharah was atop Zigazig like a man, moving her
smaller tail between the redhead's wide-spread fleshier
thighs as if she had a dong inside her and, from the way
Zigazig was moving her big hips, the redhead seemed to
think there was, too. He was still trying to figure out what
they were getting out of all that effort when Fatima
clamped down on his own questing shaft with her internal
muscles and begged him to go faster. So he did, and it was
worth it when they came together, hard.

As he lay in Fatima's arms, sated for the moment, he
looked again and, damn it, this time the big redhead was
on top and seemed to be trying to screw skinny little
Sharah to death, but with what? He asked Fatima if she
knew what was going on. She giggled and said something
in Arabic. So the redhead giggled, too, and rose from the
saddle of Sharah's thighs to show him.

He blinked and said, "I see it, but I don't believe it!
How in the fuck did Zigazig grow a cock and balls all of a
sudden?" For that was what it looked like as the redhead
lewdly stroked the heroic moist male member sticking out
from her red pubic hair. Fatima told her in Arabic to let
him have a better look. So Zigazig gave a tug, a grunt, and
held the impossible-looking object up to the light.

It was obviously made of flesh-colored rubber, on closer
inspection. Not one but two amazingly realistic eight
inchers sprouted in a Y from the base made to look like a
pair of human balls. He laughed and said, "I see how it
works, now. You girls sure must have a lot of spare time to
kill in each other's company."

Fatima sighed and said, "You Infidels have no idea.
Aside from our own men being unable to sleep with us all
at once, thanks to the Prophet's teachings that four wives
and as many harem girls as a man can afford is only right

and proper, when they *do* summon us to bed, they are seldom interested in, ah, old-fashioned loving."

"You mean it's hard for a healthy Arab girl to get a good old-fashioned screwing?"

"Not as often as a healthy woman would like, señor. You see, when a man has all the sex he could ever want at his beck and call—"

"Yeah, guys who eat too much develop jaded appetites for unusual food, too," he cut in, adding, "Jesus, I wonder how many dames I'd have to screw before I really got to wondering what a rosy-cheeked boy might be like."

"Shall we find out?" asked Fatima, adding, "Why do you not have sex with Zigazig, now, while I finish screwing Sharah?"

That sounded fair, since he'd already come in old Zigazig, albeit not the old-fashioned way. So the redhead climbed up beside him and welcomed him with open arms and wide-spread thighs as Fatima calmly squatted between Sharah's legs to insert the mock maleness, or one shaft of it, up her own freshly fornicated snatch.

Captain Gringo lost track of the rest of the gang for a while as he discovered to his surprised delight that the redhead screwed even better than she blew the French horn.

Yet despite the renewed inspiration of his new surroundings and the inspired way Zigazig moved them, it was starting to drift from pleasure into honest toil now. A man as virile as Captain Gringo was usually good for thrice in a row, even with the same woman. But thanks, or no-thanks, to his orgy with Anita earlier that same day in the deserted house, he was having a hard time getting there.

Zigazig, fortunately, took it as a gallant compliment when she came ahead of him and he just kept going. She sobbed up at him in Arabic and started writhing all over the pillows under him. That helped. He was getting there when, suddenly, littla Sharah pounced on him from behind and seemed to be trying to shove something up his ass for some reason. He told her to cut it out and when that didn't work, twisted his head around to ask Fatima what in the hell was wrong with the crazy dame.

Fatima was reclining casually off to one side, just watching as she fingered herself. She explained, "Some Spanish gentlemen seem to enjoy that particular vice. They say it gives them an enormous erection to be sodomised by a man while they make love to a woman."

He said, "Glugh. Tell her I'm neither a Spaniard nor a gentleman and if I was, I still wouldn't want a rubber dong up my bung, God damn it. Jesus, you girls act like you haven't had a man at your mercy for at least a month!"

Fatima sighed and said, "It's been longer than that. We are not allowed to service the trade with the regular whores working here. You see, Abdul feels it proper to keep the usual four wives of a rich Bedu, even though he prefers boys."

"Oh, shit, I just laid two of Gemal's *wives?*"

"Yes, I think it's Sharah's turn now. You've already been nice to Zigazig and poor little Sharah is terribly excited!"

"That's for sure," he muttered as the nutty little Sharah tried to shove her rubber dong up his ass again. He decided anything else they did together had to have *that* notion beat. So he kissed Zigazig a fond farewell, rolled off her, and grabbed Sharah to toss her across the pile of pillows on her giggling back. The synthetic male organs he hauled out of her felt silly as hell, too. He grimaced, tossed them aside, and mounted the hot little North African.

She screamed aloud as he entered her. Fatima laughed and said, "She says you are too much for her, that way. She wants to get on top so she can have something to say about how deep it goes in her."

That sounded not only fair but restful. So he rolled off Sharah and onto his own back to let her mount him, giggling at first, then grunting in apparent agony as she eased down his shaft, which for some reason seemed to be coming to life again. The fact she was tight as hell probably had something to do with that. He liked it even better when Sharah began to bounce up and down, taking it, as best he could tell, as far as it would go.

He had a better view of the others from this position. So he watched with interest as Zigazig picked up the flesh-colored double dildo to turn herself into a sort of soft-looking boy again. He was expecting her to mount Fatima, of course. But the big redhead got behind Sharah with her lush thighs forked across Captain Gringo's legs, and what happened next was just plain silly.

Sharah leaned forward, pressing her little cupcake breasts down against his chest as she arched her spine and Zigazig mounted her from the rear, dog style, or rather, since Captain Gringo was in her usual love box, Greek style. He could feel the other shaft moving inside Sharah. It felt more weird and wild than sexy, at first, but it seemed to do wonders for Sharah, and as she clamped down on his real male shaft in a series of delicious pulsations, he sighed and said, "Oh, well, when in Rome, or maybe a fucking *tent*..."

Since Zigazig's mock male movements were of course moving the other end of the crazy device in her own she-male insides as well, they party got wild indeed by the time all three of them came in one big gasping mass of quivering flesh. As he lay quietly with little Sharah's pulsing interior milking any drops left over out, Captain Gringo sighed and said, "Why thank you, God. You've been a real pal, this evening. So forget what I called you earlier in those sewers."

The door popped open and yet another naked lady dashed in. He looked her over, nodded, and said, "I guess so. If only I can ever get it up again."

But the newcomer hadn't come to join the party. She burbled at the first three in Arabic, and the next thing he knew all four of them were up and out, leaving him spreadeagled on the pillows with a limp dick, a dish of candied fruit, and a bottle of booze. So he just laughed, said, "Okay, enough is enough," and closed his eyes. He'd had a hard as well as hard-on day and he was asleep in no time.

It was too good to last. He had no idea how long he'd slept, but he sure wanted more when someone woke him up, rather rudely, by pulling on his cock as if it was a bell cord.

Captain Gringo groaned, rubbed his face, and muttered, "If you don't cut that out I'll kill you." Then he opened his eyes and added, "What the hell . . . ?"

The woman seated on the pillows, jerking him off or awake, was as naked as he was and almost as big. The face wasn't bad and she had a fantastic pair of knockers, if one didn't mind a little hair on a lady's chest. She had a slight moustache, too. But she was for sure all she-male. She forked a massive thigh across him and attempted, without much luck, to shove his wrung-out love sausage up inside her. He yawned and said, "Jesus, let a guy wake up at least. I can see you want to fuck, but who the fuck *are* you?"

She chuckled down at him and asked, "Don't you recognize me without my clothes on, Deek?"

"Does anybody? The face is familiar, but I just can't place the snatch."

"So I notice, alas. You've been eating that damned opium candy they left for you, eh?"

He glanced over at the bowl of sickly sweet candied fruit and asked, "They put *opium* in candy apples, figs, or whatever?"

"Abdul's idea," she replied, adding, "He likes to keep his guests semiconscious. It makes them easier to get along with and keeps them from fooling with his wives. You haven't been doing anything *that* dumb, have you?"

"Perish the thought. I didn't even know he was married. Last time I saw him he was kissing a colored boy."

She laughed and said, "That's probably why he's so

possessive. The poor girls are lesbians as well. They haven't much choice. They know Abdul would kill them if he caught them even flirting with a real man and . . . Hmm, speaking of real men, I do believe I detect the first signs of life down here. You like?''

He grinned up at the big broad as he said, ''I must have been asleep longer than I thought. What time is it?''

''Almost dawn. If we're going to screw, we'd better get started, don't you think?''

She had the head inside her now, and despite her size, it had no complaints about feeling lonely in wide-open spaces. He thrust with his hips and she hissed in pleasure as she felt another few inches go into her. She said, ''Oh, nice. I can't wait until it grows up. Would you like me to go down on you, pal?''

''No thanks, buddy, you're doing fine. Where did you learn to talk like a Yankee seaman with a slight Spanish accent and, come to think of it, you still haven't told me who the fuck you *are!*''

She said, ''Oh, yes, I mean to fuck you good before you get away, Deek. I make it a policy never to fuck the regulars downstairs. It can feel so awkward, beating up a lover, and . . .''

''Jesus H. Christ! You're Boca the Bouncer?''

''Who were you expecting, Her Majesty, the Queen? Actually, Abdul told me to get you and Gaston up early. He didn't say how early and so . . . well, once I'd seen you sleeping alone, naked, with such a lovely love tool lying there so lost and lonely—''

''Hey, don't try to explain,'' he cut in, thrusting in her fully awake indeed as he added, ''This beats the prettiest alarm clock they could make out of solid gold by a mile!''

''Ooffff!'' she hissed as he hit bottom for the first time. ''You seem to be beating me with a mile, or at least a foot of candy cane. Let me get on the bottom. I'm going to have to take charge before you rupture me, you brute!''

He didn't argue, but her request still struck him as an

odd one. Most dames said they wanted to be on top because they could control the pain better from that position. How in the hell did this one intend to take *charge* in the submissive position?

Boca the Bouncer showed him. She lay on her back and he mounted her as per usual. Then she drew her big legs up to brace her knees against his chest. So, okay, that did keep him from putting his full weight on her. But then Boca got her shins between them and wedged her bare feet between his thighs, cupping his balls in the insteps as her toes curled up to literally hold him in a sort of soft split-saddle, with his shaft still in her, and then Boca the Bouncer and the man she was playing Pony Boy with proceeded to bounce like hell.

He laughed incredulously and said, "Jesus, it's no wonder they call you a bouncer!" as he rode effortlessly on her insteps like a sex maniac riding a bicycle seat with his balls hanging through it and his dong in someone very nice riding double with him.

She said, "Don't talk dirty. I told you I never do this with the drunks I throw out, and by the time the joint closes the few guys Abdul might have staying overnight have usually overindulged in Abdul's opium or freak collection. I can see you haven't been at the dope or any of the dopey whores or queers I was afraid might have gotten at you first. Jesus, you've grown since I first met you!"

He laughed and asked, "How can you tell? You don't have all of me in you. She said, "Half a meatloaf is better than one when a girl's as petite as me. Are you saying you don't enjoy doing it this way?"

"Well, I must say it's a novelty," said Captain Gringo, too polite to add he *couldn't* have done it this way with a normal woman. How many women, or even men, had legs that long and strong? It felt crazy as hell just sitting on her feet while she used his whole far-from-light body to jerk herself off with. But it was having the same effect on him as Boca bounced him in and out of her now passionate love box with no effort at all on his part, save from hanging on to her knees to avoid being bucked off and out. But thanks to earlier adventures she attributed to opium, thank God, the sex-starved giantess was getting there ahead of him and as she suddenly moaned, "Oh, I can't stand it. Stop teasing me and do it *right,* you brute!" he was able to do so, thanks to his restful ride in her cuntry. Boca spread her thighs and then spread them some more, since she had so much thigh to spread, and as he tried to mount her like a proper little hentleman, she seized him in a bear hug and hauled him down upon and into her, holding him in a viselike grip, everywhere she had a hold on him. He could barely breathe, let alone move his hips enough to matter once she'd wrapped her massive legs around him as well. But that worked out all right, in her end, since Boca the Bouncer bounced great that way, too. As she did all the work, bumping and grinding under him like a man-killing bronc, but holding him safely in her love saddle with her powerful arms and legs, Boca sobbed, "Oh, you're so brutal! You're killing me with your savage thrusting lust, but I'm helpless in your arms and, yes, yes, yessss, *take* me, you animal!"

He sure did, although it was hard not to laugh at the same time, knowing the Victorian under-the-counter novel she'd gotten all that bullshit out of. But what the hell, the poor lonesome gal didn't get to meet many guys who could have survived her coy lovemaking, so she probably got to read alone in bed a lot.

She came again ahead of him, protesting he was making her feel used and abused. Then he ejaculated in her, harder than he'd expected to, and she felt it, gasping, "Oh, my God, how could you have done such a thing *inside* me, Deek?"

He laughed and said, "It was easy. You were doing all the work. Didn't you *expect* me to come, sooner or later?"

"Of course, but not *inside* me! It's a sin to go all the

way when you're not married! A *gentleman* is supposed to
pull it out at the last minute!''

"Jesus, I didn't come here tonight to be insulted. I gave
up being a gentleman long ago, but does anybody listen
and, ah, by the way, if you want me to take it out, how
come we're still bouncing like this, Boca?''

"I'm trying to teach you how merely courting couples
are supposed to make love, of course. Tell me when you
are about to come again. I am, ah, sort of busy right now.''

She could have said that again, but as she bounced him
in her even harder and faster, Boca was too overcome with
passion for conversation, which was just as well, since she
talked awfully dumb for a dame who screwed so good. He
wasn't sure, now, whether he was enjoying himself or
getting sea sick. Making love to Boca the Bouncer was a
lot like riding a roller coaster or a ship at sea in a storm.

But the big soft broad was a lot softer and yummier than
anything else he'd ever ridden that moved so violently. The
effortless thrusts in her smooth wet warm interior might
have kept a corpse with a hard-on if it had ever had any
feelings at all. He wasn't sure how or if Boca would notice
the difference if he died on top of her right now. He
deliberately lay limp in her arms, not trying to even keep it
in, as she moved faster and faster, sobbing, "Oh, not
again! Have you no feelings, Deek? How can you keep
doing this to me, over and over, without even giving me a
chance to catch my breath? What are you, a man or a
machine?''

He growled, "I'm a big steam pile driver, my proud
helpless beauty! Too long have you evaded my unholy
desires and now, if you don't surrender yourself to me I
mean to tie you down to the railroad tracks and screw you
till the Pacific Flier thunders down on us, going puffatapuffata
as we die, creamed in one another's arms beneath its cruel
steel wheels!''

He thought he was joshing her and her reading material.
But Boca sighed, "Oh, you're so romantic! I feel so

helpless and little as you vent your lust in my all too weak flesh!''

This time he had to laugh. But she didn't notice as she added, "Oh, oh, God help me, I can't resist any longer! I'm cominggggg!''

That made two of them, or it ould have, had not Boca suddenly gasped, "No! Don't you *dare!* Let me show you how to come with a lady!''

He had nothing to say about it as she ejected his shaft like a watermelon seed with a powerful internal contraction, hauled him up her smooth and now sweaty torso as if he was a rag doll, and as he just let her toss him around, to see what on earth she had in mind, Boca sat him on her lower chest, shoved his confused erection between her moist, massive breasts, and said, "There, finish *that* way!'' as she pressed her big mamma-mias together, encasing his privates in the resultant tight crease between them.

Stimulated by the novelty, he started moving back and forth on her chest, using her breasts as a surprisingly interesting substitute for the real thing. Boca laughed, raised her head from the pillows, and giggled, saying, "Oh, I can see the head of it peeking in and out of my titties at me. Are you ready to come that way, Deek?''

"I might be, if you'd just shut up and *let* me!''

"I don't want you coming on my chest. It feels icky Could you move up a little, Deek?''

He did, hugging her massive rib cage with his thighs as he kept fornicaing her knockers. But now, damn it, most of him was thrusting out the far side. So he was about to move back, when Boca cranked her head higher and kissed the throbbing head of his dong, saying, "Farther, just a little farther,'' until suddenly he had half of it between her slippery breasts and the other more important half between her tightly pursed lips. So when he came, and he did, hard, it was not on her chest. He gasped, fell limply sideways, and just lay there, wondering where he was, as Boca rolled after him, still sucking. He'd already found out why "Bouncer" fit her. Now he could see "Boca" did, as well, since Boca meant mouth in Spanish. He'd assumed when they'd met she was a *loud* mouth. He liked educational surprises. But he protested, "No shit, honey. Enough is enough. I have a boat to catch and at this rate they'll have to carry me up the gangplank!"

She raised her head from his lap to grin roguishly down at him and say, "Hah, I just licked Captain Gringo!"

He laughed weakly and said, "You call that licking? It felt more like sucking to me. But okay, I surrender. You fight dirty, but what the hell, I like it."

Before she could tell him the penalty for losing, the door opened and Gaston said, "Ah, there you are, Dick. I see you and Boca have met. I hate to be a spoilsport, mais that swishy black of Abdul's is waiting for us downstairs and he apparently expects us to either cornhole him or follow him to the ship. My Arabic is getting rusty."

Boca the Bouncer swore like a sailor in three languages, but let Captain Gringo sit up and even helped him find his clothes among the loose pillows as the big but now weak-kneed American asked Gaston about their papers. Gaston patted his jacket and said, "Oui, très artistic, too. You are a M'sieur DuVal and I must be an Irishman unless McBride is a Jewish name. The forger seems to have gotten our descriptions mixed up. But no matter, very few customs officials can read English and that is what the supercargo licenses are made out in, hein?"

Captain Gringo laughed, finished dressing, and rose weakly with the aid of both his friends. Only Boca insisted on kissing him at the door. She didn't follow, since lady bouncers looked silly in the nude on the stairs.

By the time they were down them, Captain Gringo was feeling at least able to walk unaided. Gaston chuckled and asked, "Hard night?"

"If I told you you'd accuse me of making it up. How did you make out, Gaston?"

"Outside," the Frenchman warned softly. So neither

said another word until they joined the black mariposa out front. He spoke neither Spanish nor English and led the way with a point and a flounce of his head and hips. So as they followed him down the quay, Gaston felt safe to explain, "I had a call of closeness. One of Abdul's wives, Marib, most treacherously neglected to tell me who she was until I had given her a French lesson and a Greek one as well. Arab women love it up the derrière. Come to think of it, so do Arab men."

"Never mind that. Was this Marib a little pale-skinned critter with big almond eyes and henna-stained nipples?"

"She was indeed! Don't tell me she crept into *your* tent, too!"

"Only to warn the other three about something. I never found out what. They all took off like scalded cats."

Gaston nodded and said, "As well they should have. Arab men are allowed to screw other women, bugger boys, and, merde, suck off sheep if they want to. But the penalty for an Arab *woman* cheating on her lord and master is death, très sure, mais *slow!*"

"Sure, in Arab countries, but this is Costa Rica, right?"

"Right and wrong, Dick. No doubt the adorable Hispanic police would frown on a woman being tortured to death on their beat, if they *knew* about it. But Abdul El Gemal is a man who deals in secret assassination by profession. At any rate, he is usually doped to the gills and sound asleep by sundown, so perhaps his Marib thought it safe to visit an even older man she admired. But for some reason, last night, the species of Arabian insect was up and about and wondering, très loudly, where in the fuck his wives might be fucking."

Captain Gringo whistled softly and said, "Oh well, all's well that ends well. We'd have probably heard the screams if the girls hadn't gotten away with it. But how did your Marib find out in time if she was playing house with you, Gaston?"

"Boca the Bouncer told us, of course. She popped in to

say the boss had sent her to look for the girls. At which point Marib lost all interest in me, alas.''

Captain Gringo chuckled indulgently and said, ''Well, at least you got laid first. Sorry the rest of the night was so dull for you.''

Gaston frowned and asked, ''Dull? How can you say that, after you just had some of Boca the Bouncer, too?''

Captain Gringo scowled thoughtfully as they followed the mincing Negro in the pale gray light of dawn. Gaston asked, ''What's wrong, are you annoyed at me for getting in there first? Le Bon Dieu knows you've made me take sloppy seconds often enough!''

''I'm not worried about that. I didn't eat any of them. But have you ever had the feeling people have been fibbing to you, Gaston?''

''Often. And we are only talking about the women in the House of Abdul, not Abdul himself, hein?''

''That's what I mean. Boca wasn't sent by the boss to round up those cheating dames. She just wanted in on the action and she sure as hell got it, or gave it. But screw the dames.''

''We just did.''

''I mean, if nobody anywhere near Gemal tells the truth, how the hell can we believe Gemal himself?''

Gaston sighed and said, ''We can't. He's probably lying to us about the entire set-up. Mais on the other hand, what other choices do we have? We are cooked, for certain, if we stay here. The odds are only ten to one against us if we accept his offer, non?''

There wasn't one woman aboard the rusty run-down banana boat as it steamed out of the harbor. So the voyage up the Mosquito Coast should have been anticlimatic if not downright dull. It began sedately enough for Captain

Gringo. Once they were safely out to sea he retired to the dinky cabin he and Gaston had been assigned to catch up on his sleeping. As usual he'd elected to sleep in the top bunk. It was annoying to sleep under the sagging bedsprings of a dirty old man who masturbated shamelessly and often. Gaston, of course, hadn't been leading as active a life of late and insisted on prowling the ship while the sun was shining. No knockaround gent was about to sleep in strange surroundings behind an unlocked door. So as Gaston left, Captain Gringo told him not to come back for a while, God damn it, and bolted the door after him.

He stripped and climbed up into his bunk, hanging the strap of his gun rig from a handy wall hook near the head of it. The porthole was tiny, but open, and as they'd lucked on to a windward cabin, the trades blew in across the cubbyhole cabin and out the transom atop the door. He stretched luxuriously and was asleep in no time. He was too wrung out to dream anything at all wet, so he had to settle for the usual nightmares of a man on the run with a price on his head.

Nightmares didn't bother Captain Gringo, the former First Lieutenant Richard Walker, U.S. 10th Cav, as much as they bothered people who led less interesting lives. Since he'd crossed the Mexican border one jump ahead of the army hangman's noose after being court martialed for a crime he'd never committed, Captain Gringo, as he'd soon been dubbed by admiring and not-so-admiring Hispanics, had been in many a situation, wide awake, that had your average nightmare whipped like a pup. As he tossed and turned on his bunk between spells of deeper much-needed rest, he was able to cope with the bullshit his dream machinery kept churning out as fast as it came out.

An ogre popped out of an otherwise pretty New England meadow he was striding across, naked, for some reason, and in his dream Captain Gringo just smiled pleasntly and said, "Get the fuck out of my way, ogre. I'm not going to say it twice."

The ogre growled, "Hijo de cabrone, you do not have your machine gun. You do not have your pistola. Shit, man, you don't even have your pants on! I've been waiting for a chance to eat the famous Captain Gringo!"

The dreaming American shook his head and said, "Sorry, I only let women, pretty ones, suck my dong." Then, since the ogre was still standing there, Captain Gringo proceeded to tear his arms and legs off like daisy petals, muttering, "You call yourself an ogre? Shit, you don't even have a guerrilla army and a mountain fortress to call your own, like the last ogre I ran into in my eternal quest for peace, quiet, and a good cigar."

As he walked on across the meadow, trying to remember where he was going, the torn-off head of the ogre called after him, "Nyah nyah, you got no clothes on and everybody's going to laugh at you in church!"

Captain Gringo started to point out he was nowhere near any church. But suddenly he was, though nobody in the pews all around seemed to have noticed yet that he was standing in the aisle stark naked. The little old nun came over to him and whispered, "You are late, my son. The ceremony was about to start without you. Come, take my arm, por favor."

He did, not knowing what else to do, as he hoped she wouldn't say anything about his full frontal nudity. She didn't. Now they were moving down the aisle toward the people waiting by the altar and though he couldn't see her face under that white veil his bride to be sure had a nice figure and . . . hadn't she been a little old nun just a minute ago? And how come they were getting married? He didn't even know her name or what she looked like. But now they were at the altar and the priest, a heavy-set mestizo wearing a big black sombrero and crossed ammo belts over his sweaty cotton shirt, was saying, "Do you, Ricardo, take this woman for to be your lawfully wedded mujer, to keep her, to cherish her, and all that bullshit?"

"Ah, padre, there's something I'd better tell you."

"Shut up, or I'll tell everyone here you are not wearing any pants and they will all laugh at you. I now pronounce you man and wife. You may kiss the bride."

"Hold it! I don't even *know* this lady, padre!"

"Sure you do. You have made love to her many many times, and now it is time for you to make an honest woman of her. Don't you wish for to kiss your one true love, Captain Gringo? Do you want us all to think you are a fairy?"

Captain Gringo turned to his bride with a shrug, moved closer, and lifted the veil to kiss her. But he screamed in his sleep instead when he saw who he'd married. The grinning skull under the bridal veil was fuzzy with grave-yard mold and gun muzzles gleamed from each otherwise empty eye socket. Her voice was like the creaking of rusty hinges opening a door into a tomb as she asked him reproachfully, "What is the matter, darling? Don't you find me beautiful, after courting me so long?"

He didn't ask her name. He didn't have to. He decided to wake up instead. He lay quietly for a time, staring at the low ceiling as he debated with his still tired body whether it was going back to sleep after a pisser like that last one.

The matter was settled for him when he heard Gaston's coded door knock. He growled, "Yeah, yeah, coming" as he rolled off the bunk. It was still light outside, whatever the hell time it was, but he felt a lot stronger now as he moved to open the door. Gaston popped in, grinned up at him, and said, "You look adorable when you are angry. I am sorry if I disturbed your beauty rest, but we seem to have a problem."

Captain Gringo bolted the door again and sat on Gaston's lower bunk, rubbing his face awake as he asked, "So what else is new? We've had a problem since we escaped that Mexican firing squad together. It's called staying alive a few more hours."

Gaston remained standing, fishing out a smoke, as he said, "I don't regard this one as life threatening. Annoying, perhaps. Mais on the other hand, we could always use the money.''

"Is there any point to this conversation, Gaston?''

Gaston lit his cigar before he shook out the match and replied, ''Oui, did you get a good look at the other, ah, passengers aboard this adorable bucket of bolts as we clambered aboard, Sleeping Beauty?''

Captain Gringo shrugged and said, ''I just made sure nobody was pointing a gun at me. I make the others the Cuba Libre guys have recruited along with us the usual collection of knockaround gents, good, bad, and who cares.''

"One of them is Turk Malone. You have heard of him, of course?''

"Not recently. Wasn't he mixed up in that not so well-run coup down Bolivia way a while back? How come he's still alive?''

"That is easy. He's tough. Before he took early retirement from your U.S. Navy, something to do with murdering an officer, Malone was the boxing champ of the Pacific Fleet.''

"Yeah, so?''

"So now he wants to arrange a boxing match with *you*.''

Captain Gringo frowned at the floor and asked, ''What the hell for? I've never even met the bastard and if he says I stole his girl he's nuts.''

Gaston shrugged and said, ''His reasons are probably financial. He thinks it would be an easy way to raise money if the two of you held an exhibition match on the well deck. Each passenger to contribute a modest amount to the kitty, the winner splitting their winnings with those who bet on him, see?''

"I'm beginning to. What does the *loser* get?''

"Merde, of course. It would be bareness of knuckles, fight to the finish, winner-take-all. I told him I would discuss the matter with you, hein?''

Captain Gringo shook his head and said, ''You've discussed

it with me and it sounds disgusting. So you can march right back and tell him I said no deal.''

"He's going to think you are a sissy, Dick.''

"So what? I think he's an asshole, and is he losing any sleep over it? I'm a professional soldier, not a prize fighter, damn it.''

"True, mais you do have a certain reputation for toughness among others in the trade. That is why Turk thinks fighting you would generate enough interest for a handsome purse.''

"It *thinks*, too? We're on our way to a goddamn battle zone. There's no telling how soon we'll be going into action, I hope on the same side. Would you like to advance on enemy guns with a guy you'd just kicked the shit out of maybe behind you, with a gun of his own?''

"Mais non. Fortunately I appear so harmless few people wish to shoot me in the back at such times.''

"That's what I just said. If I licked Turk, I'd have to worry about him letting me down in combat. If he licked me, he'd worry the same way whether he'd have to or not. Neither of us would be able to do his best, and the Spanish Army must have a *few* good soldiers in its ranks. So tell Turk thanks, but no thanks. What time is it?''

"Almost the hour of cenar. We'll all be eating together in the ship's mess. Are you prepared to eat with men who may have you down as a coward, Dick?''

"I'm prepared to eat with Jack the Ripper if only he'll keep his knife out of my plate. I'm hungry as a bitch wolf. You got me into this, so go get me out of it while I dress. I'll join you when I hear the dinner gong. I know where the mess is.''

Gaston left. Captain Gringo moved to the tiny sink built into one corner and inspected his face in the cracked mirror above it as he pissed in it. He could use a shave. But the tap water was saline as well as cold, and he didn't expect to meet Miss Lillie Langtry in the ship's mess. So what the hell. He wet one corner of a towel, brushed his teeth with it, then gave himself a whore bath with sea water and some sort of soap that didn't seem to want to dissolve in it much.

He hauled on his shirt and pants, stomped on his mosquito boots, and stood undecided for a minute as he considered his gun rig. Then he strapped it on over his shirt. Guns were like dames and money. A guy could never have too many, too much, or tell in advance when he'd be hurting for 'em. He put his linen jacket on over the shoulder holster to be polite. He'd lost his damned hat somewhere in his recent travels, but nobody but Orthodox Jews and cowhands came to the table with their hats on, so why worry?

By the time he was presentable someone was beating a dinner bell or at least a frying pan in the distance. So he sallied forth to meet the rest of the passenger list and crew.

Gaston met him first, in the doorway of the ship's mess. Six other men were already seated at the long bare table, waiting to be fed. Only one, a big moronic guy with crooked teeth and sandy hair, was looking their way as Gaston quickly murmured, "Turk Malone is the moose at the head of the table, profile to us. I told him. He did not seem happy about it. The consumptive-looking individual in the seersucker jacket is Ace Cavendish, professional gambler, professional killer, depending on the stakes. The burly caveman with the eyebrows that meet in the middle is Bully Baker, not a bad sort if one does not ask if his mother really escaped from a zoo."

"Who's the sandy-haired punk with the knowing sneer?"

"Oh, that is Reb Ritter, born in a très piney part of Alabama, and no doubt he should have stayed there. But they hang men in Alabama for rape, so, like us, he gets by the best way he can. He's been in more waterfront brawls than revolutions, but like Turk he survived that disaster in Bolivia. So he must be doing *something* right, hein?"

"He looks like an asshole."

"He is. A nasty one. The other two are Tex Thatcher and Rimfire McGraw, both no doubt better cowboys than soldiers of fortune, but when a man is wanted by the law in your très fussy States he does the best he can to get by. Shall we join our fellow adventurers?''

They did. Gaston introduced Captain Gringo all around. Nobody said anything nasty at first, but nobody offered to shake hands. Turk Malone, the Pacific champ, even managed a nod that was neither friendly nor hostile. Captain Gringo decided to keep an eye on him anyway. The son of a bitch was *big!*

An Hispanic mess boy came out of the galley and began to distribute the food. As they dug in, Gaston told Captain Gringo the ship's cook was a Chinaman. The tall American nodded and said, ''It figures. It's not bad grub.''

Across the table, the sandy-haired Reb Ritter grinned foolishly and said, in a mocking falsetto, ''Oh, isn't that grand, gents? The Damnyankee approves of our supper!'' Then he added in a deeper tone, ''I was old enough to screw wimmen afore I larnt Damnyankee wasn't one word, Walker.''

Captain Gringo nodded pleasantly and replied, ''That's fair. I was shaving regular by the time I learned Robert E. Lee wasn't a steamboat.''

Reb Ritter looked astounded and announced, ''Whooooo-heeee! This here Damnyankee acts like it's got hair on its chest! Ain't that a bitch? I thought all Damnyankees set down to pee, but this one's trying to talk like a *man!* Are you a real man, Yankee Boy? You don't look like a real man to me. You look like a she-boy who's been practicing in front of a mirror to *talk* like one.''

Captain Gringo snorted in disgust and asked, ''Is there any point to this bullshit, Ritter? I signed on to fight the Spanish, not the Civil War. And for the record, my dad was too old for the Civil War, and they said I couldn't join up until I learned to walk and talk at least.''

Ritter scowled and said, ''Hey, watch that Civil War shit, Yankee! Where I comes from it's calt the War Betwixt the States, hear?''

"Where I come from some old farts still call it the Great Rebellion. But neither of us are where we come from, so eat your supper like a good little boy and let's say no more about it."

Reb Ritter laughed mockingly and called up the table, "Hey, Turk, what do you make of this here Yankee Boy? I thought he was supposed to be afeared to fight, yet he's sassing me shamefull!"

The massive Malone went on cutting his steak as he growled, "Watch it, Junior. Man said he didn't want to fight. He never said he didn't know *how*."

Captain Gringo was beginning to suspect he'd been worried about the wrong guy as Ritter turned back to him to ask, "That right, Yankee Boy? Could you be hiding unsuspected talents ahint that sissy face of your'n?"

Captain Gringo didn't answer. The Texan seated next to Ritter moved his plate farther away, shaking his head in silent weariness.

Captain Gringo decided Tex Thatcher was probably a real fighter despite his modest rep. Real fighters knew better than to get mixed up in fights they didn't *have* to. A man *got* to be a real fighter by getting licked a few times, and knowing after that how filled with surprises life could be.

The main course was filling, the coffee was good, so Captain Gringo decided to skip the dessert, if any. As he rose from the table Ritter called after him, "Hey, don't go 'way mad, honey! Come back here and tell us how tough you are some more."

Captain Gringo walked out on deck, found a handy hatch cover, and sat on it to enjoy an after-dinner claro. The sun was setting over to the west now, outlining the mangrove-haunted shoreline they were steaming along like black Spanish lace against crimson satin. The sea was calm, more reddish than green in the sunset light, and from time to time a flying fish drew an arc of water turned to gleaming gold above the gentle waves. Captain Gringo had always liked this time of the day. It always seemed to end too soon.

In this case, his peaceful mood was broken by the others coming out on deck to join him, belching and lighting their own smokes.

Most of them had been down here long enough to have adopted the sensible Hispanic habit of never sitting down next to anyone uninvited. They'd all seen cantina fights started by no more than a drunk plopping down across the table from a man he didn't know quite well. So Reb Ritter was obviously still looking for a fight when he sat down beside Captain Gringo and said, "My, ain't this sunset romantical, Yankee Boy? Tell me something, Yankee Boy, if I was to court you proper, would you take it in the ass for me, or do Damnyankees only suck? I really want to know. For I'm just a poor old country boy who's never fucked nothing uglier than a nigger, but I'm willing to *larn*, hear?"

Captain Gringo sighed and said, "I read someplace that lots of natural bullies suffer from a hidden homosexual streak. Wife beaters, too. You must have interesting dreams, Reb."

"I'll dream you, you mealy-mouthed Damnyankee! Where do you get off low-rating me with fancy professor words long enough to stick in the ground for bean poles? Was you trying to call me a sissy boy just now? If you was a *man*, you'd just come right out and say what you *meant*, hear?"

Captain Gringo was aware nobody else was talking now as he weighed his own words and said, "All right. Since you don't seem to have figured it out yourself yet, you're an asshole, Reb. We signed on to fight a war with Spain, not one another."

"Mebbe so. But them's fighting words just the same, Damnyankee, and anyone who calls me an asshole owes me a trip to Fist City. So let's get on with it, hear?"

Captain Gringo shook his head and said, "No thanks. Let's just say you win and spare all the sweat and bother. I didn't come aboard to fight you. I don't want to fight you. So that's that.''

"Haw! You're afeared of me, aint you?''

"If you say so. Shit, for all I care, you can say Grant surrendered to Lee at Appomattox, Reb. We just don't have anything sensible to fight about and, oh hell, I'm going back to bed.''

He meant it. He stood up and turned away. Then both Gaston and Turk Malone, of all people, shouted the same warning. So Captain Gringo turned just as Reb Ritter swung. The warming saved him from catching the round-house punch with the nape of his neck, which could have killed him. But it didn't save him from catching it with his jaw, which didn't feel so great either!

Captain Gringo reeled back from the staggering blow and would have fallen had not his back crashed into a cabin bulkhead. His legs felt like empty wading boots under him and the space between him and the man who'd cold-cocked him was filled with a pinwheeling galaxy of little stars. But he stayed on his feet. Then he wondered why anyone would want to do a dumb thing like that as Ritter bored in, landing punch after punch despite the dazed victim's feeble attempts to block them with a pair of arms that felt heavy as lead.

Then Turk Malone had Ritter from behind and was hauling him off, saying, "He's had enough, and that was dirty, kid. The man said he didn't want to fight and you hit him from behind!''

Ritter yelled, "Just lemme go so's I can hit him agin, damn it! The fight ain't over. He never went *down*. Just lemme lay him on the ground once, so's I can say he went down. I won't stomp him, honest!''

Captain Gringo shook his head to clear it, noticed most of the stars seemed to have flown somewhere else, and moved his weight from side to side to get some blood back in his legs as he said very quietly, "Let him go, Turk.''

The professional boxer grunted, "Not yet. You're still hurt, kid."

"I noticed. Let him go, anyway."

Malone shrugged and told Ritter, "If you've got any sense at all, start *running!*" and unwrapped his apelike arms to free the man who'd just cold-cocked Captain Gringo. It was darker now. Somewhere in the gloom, Tex Thatcher said quietly, "I got fifty dollars says the Yank will whup his ass."

There were no takers. Captain Gringo had fallen into a boxer's crouch but was waiting to see what Ritter meant to do next. Ritter seemed to be having second thoughts now that he'd given the Damnyankee his best shot, from behind, and the man who should have been down *there* was still up *here!* He licked his lips and said, "Aw, shoot, I'm willing to call it a draw, Walker."

Captain Gringo said flatly, "I'm not." Then, since the mountain didn't seem willing to come to Mohammed, Captain Gringo was gliding forward in a fighting crouch, dukes up, with less expression on his face than a tobbaconist ordering a wooden Indian would be willing to pay for. As Ritter backed away from him across the well deck, Turk Malone nudged Gaston and said, "You told me your boy had never boxed professionally. Were you trying to set me up, you sneaky little Frog?"

"Eh bien, perhaps he had some instruction in the sport at West Point. I assure you he never fights for money, avec his *fists!*"

Captain Gringo feinted with his right and decked Ritter with his first thrown punch, a left hook.

Malone said, "He'd make a fortune if he did."

Rimfire McGraw, despite his own Southern background, yelled, "Stomp him, Yank! He's got it comin' after doing you dirty! Kick his fool haid in! He's a disgrace to the Stars and Bars!"

Captain Gringo did no such thing. He backed away,

saying, "All right, Reb. Are you going to get up or do I have to pick you up?"

"I give! I give!" whined the man on the deck, wiping at the blood running down his chin as he added, "You whupped me square and it's over, hear?"

Captain Gringo shook his head and said, "We're playing by your own rules, Reb. Saying you don't want to fight isn't good enough. Last time I tried that some cocksucker hit me anyway, from behind, and now it's *your* turn! If it's any comfort to you, I'm fighting you fair. But *I'll* tell *you* when this fight is over, and shit, you still owe me *lots* of punches, Reb!"

Turk Malone called out, "Get up, Reb. If he won't stomp you, I will. I told you not to mess with him. But you did, dirty, and it's time to pay the piper, like it or not."

"He's too good for me, Turk!"

"You just noticed? Get up, Reb. You started it. Me and the boys are anxious to see how you mean to finish it, and so far, you're putting on a piss-poor performance for the crowd."

There was an ominous growl of agreement from the others. Tex Thatcher announced, "Ten dollars say he's too yaller to git up." Ace Cavendish said, "You're on. For just this one time."

Tex lost. With a sudden howl of mingled fear and shame Reb Ritter leaped to his feet and put up his dukes. But not empty. Gaston reached for his own blade as he snapped, "Dick, regard the cochon's left hoof!"

"I see it," said Captain Gringo, adding, "Everyone else stay out of this. Come on, Reb, you've got your little pig sticker out. Let's see you stick this little pig!"

Ritter charged, leading with his right, the six-inch blade held closer in, ready to strike like an adder's tongue at the first opening. Captain Gringo dropped his guard to offer one. Ritter took him up on it, reversing his stance to lead with the knife. Captain Gringo sucked in his gut as the blade stabbed forward. Then he had Ritter's knife hand by the wrist with his own left hand. He yanked him forward, off balance, grabbed Ritter's locked left elbow from behind, and shoved hard. Elbows were not designed to bend that way. Ritter's didn't, until something gave with a sickening snap and Captain Gringo, having thoughtfully braced his own right heel on the deck across Ritter's shin, tossed him head first into the scuppers with a broken arm. For a man who claimed to be so tough, Ritter sounded amazingly like a woman screaming in childbirth as he writhed against the bulwark calling for his mother, a doctor, or somebody, to make it stop hurting him so bad.

Up on the bridge a Spanish-speaking crew member called down to ask what all the noise down there was all about. Gaston called back in the same language, "The boys are just fooling around. Nothing we can't handle!" Then he turned to the others and asked in a softer tone, "Eh bien, how are we to handle it?"

Turk Malone said, "Easy. A coward with a busted flipper ain't no good to nobody." Then he bent over, picked Ritter up by the hair and belt, and as both Ritter and Captain Gringo shouted, "No!" threw the screaming Reb over the side!

There was a moment of stunned silence, punctuated by a splash and what may have been a soggy scream from somewhere far below. The bridge called down again to ask what in the hell they were *doing* down there and this time Turk replied in Spanish, "Just getting rid of some trash, skipper. It's all over."

Captain Gringo hadn't been so sure it was over. So he'd moved out to the middle of the well deck to give himself more room as he slipped off his jacket and waited warily to see if anyone else wanted a piece of the action. Ace Cavendish was the one closest to him now, so it was Ace who said, "For God's sake, he's been packing a *gun* all this time!"

Turk Malone moved closer, stared soberly at the man he'd once been dumb enough to challenge to a fight, and said, "Right. How come you took a chance with your bare hands against that knife, kid? Didn't your folks ever tell you it smarts to have your belly ripped open?"

Captain Gringo shrugged and said, "I told him I'd give him a fair fight. He only pulled a knife on me, not a gun."

Turk nodded soberly and said, "Remind me never to pull a gun on you, either. You're okay, Walker. I still think I could take you in ten rounds, Queensbury. But I sure don't want to fight with you *unfriendly*!"

They shook on it. Ace told Tex he'd like that ten spot now, and Tex paid without argument. So it was beginning to look as if Captain Gringo had fallen among gentlemen after all. Nobody would ever mention Reb Ritter's name again.

The hitherto sleepy and still out-of-the-way Mexican seaport of Progreso could be described by the time they arrived there in one word: crowded. It reminded Captain Gringo of a gold-rush town in the West he'd known in his U.S. Army days, save for the Spanish architecture and lush tropic vegetation sprouting where it still could. But the unpaved streets were rutted and puddled by traffic they'd never been designed for, and most of the crowd was costumed for, say, Tombstone or Silver City.

As he followed Gaston and the others down the gangplank, someone in the distance was plunking "My Cherokee Rose" on a banjo, and the trio of hombres waiting to greet them on the quay didn't look like Mexicans or even Cubans. They looked like they'd just held up the Union Pacific. All three were Anglo Saxon of feature, ten gallon of hat, and armed to the teeth. Their buscadero gun belts and six guns made sense anywhere south of the border. But Captain Gringo couldn't help wondering what sort of a town Progreso was when he noted the twelve-gauge sawed-off shotguns each of them carried as well.

The leader of the delegation was a tall, lean, middle-aged gent who described himself as Colonel Hiram Scroggs, late of the Army of Virginia. Captain Gringo didn't think it wise to tell him he had to be full of shit. Scroggs hardly seemed old enough to have served as a field-grade officer in any war that had ended thirty years ago. But he might have made a couple of stripes as a pretty young Johnny Reb, and he didn't look like a man who'd take being called a liar well.

The "Colonel" introduced his back-up as Major Morgan Royce, late of Her Majesty's Indian Rifles, and Captain Sean O'Hara, who'd made *his* supposed rank in the Irish Fenian Movement, Sligo Brigade.

Captain Gringo didn't tell them they were full of shit, either. Royce was big for a Welshman and if Irishmen came any bigger and meaner looking than O'Hara he wanted them on his side, too.

After they'd all shaken hands and congratulated one another on looking so tough Scroggs said, "We was told to expect eight of you boys. I only see seven. How come?"

Turk Malone said, "What you see is what you get. Somebody must have made a mistake." And though Captain Gringo and the others off the banana boat got it and saw Turk was only telling the simple truth, nobody but Rimfire snickered. He was still new to the game.

Scroggs shrugged and said, "Well, seven's better than none, I reckon. Some friendly greasers tell us tales of Mex Rurales skulking in the jungles all around. You boys will want to draw your front money and weapons, and we've quartered you as well as this shitty one-hoss town can manage. Let's see, now . . . You two stick with me. You three go with O'Hara, here. Walker, we got a Maxim covered with axle grease you'll be wanting to strip and clean and I hear Verrier here is your sidekick and armorer. So you two'd best go with Royce, here."

The Welshman nodded and motioned Captain Gringo and Gaston to follow him. So they did. As they strode down the shady side of the calle side by side Royce said, "You'd both better wear some sidearms the next time you see fit to step out of your quarters. The natives are restless, you see."

Captain Gringo said, "We're already packing double-action .38s in shoulder rigs, Major." But Royce shook his head and said, "Not good enough, look you. It's not enough to *be* well armed in Progreso. If you don't wish to kill a local every hour on the hour you have to *look* well armed. These greasers are like children. They have to be kept in their place. And most of them don't know about shoulder holsters. When they see a nice pair of boots walking about without a gun they know of . . . Why am I telling you lads this? You've both been in this part of the world longer than I have, look you!"

That seemed obvious, but neither soldier of fortune commented. If Royce lived long enough he'd learn how to get along with Latin Americans, or in this case probably local Indians, better. A lot of the trouble people unfamiliar with Latin customs got into in this part of the world was based on mutual ignorance. One could hardly expect the less educated natives of any country to understand the customs of strangers. So it was up to the strangers to understand what was considered normal local behavior and what was considered stepping on local toes. For openers, very few Spanish-speaking people liked to be called greasers. On the other hand, many a good-natured gringo, looking for no more than a hot tamale or at most a friendly lay, could mistake good-humored Mexican joshing for an invitation to a duel. Captain Gringo said, "We know how to get along with Mexicans, unless they're Rurales or Federales. Not even Mexicans can get along with *those* mothers. Where are you quartering us, Major?"

Royce said, "Big clean house, owned by some kind of Yankee naturalist, down here to study the local flora and fauna, she says. Frankly I think she's a bit bonkers, but harmless, and as I said the suite of rooms we've issued you are clean and the food she serves should be more digestible than most of our lads have been eating of late."

Captain Gringo frowned thoughtfully and asked, "You say you, or the rebel forces, have quartered us on this American woman? What did *she* have to say about it?"

Royce shrugged and replied, "What *could* she have had to say about it? She did raise a bit of a fuss, come to think of it, until we pointed out how much better off she'd be with a pair of armed men posted inside her house instead of trying to break in, full of rum and no doubt anxious to know in the Biblical sense one of the only white women living alone in Progreso."

"That must have made her think twice. What does she look like?"

"A dog. She must be at least forty and looks like a spinster nanny, which she is, in a way. Keeps a bloody zoo of wild and domestic beasts out back and spends most of her time petting and feeding them. She won't be any bother to you. Do you want me to requisition some better-looking adelitas for you, if you want to enjoy more reasonable sex?"

"We usually find our own, thanks. But what do you mean requisition, Major? That's an unusual way to put fixing a pal up, isn't it?"

Royce shook his head and said, "Not in Progreso. I just told you. Most of the locals are a bit surly and when you just whistle at one of the mujeres they run inside and slam the bloody door in your face. So when one of our men wants to get laid we simply tell the alcalde to round up something nice and send it over, look you."

The two soldiers of fortune exchanged glances. Gaston said, "Forgive me, perhaps I am dense. But did not someone say this was an army of *liberation*?"

Royce nodded and said, "Right. Soon as we're up to full strength it's off to Cuba to liberate the little brown buggers. Meanwhile we're here in Mexico, and nobody's paying us to liberate anyone in *Mexico*. Some of the local women aren't bad, if you don't mind moon faces and somewhat darker ass than one finds back in Blighty. It's a matter of military discipline. Even the local government had to agree, once we pointed it out to them, that it's better to issue field whores to an army than have them running about raping on their own. It's all handled quite proper. The alcalde selects local girls who are no doubt no more than they should be and, meanwhile, his own wife and daughters are safe. The General has issued strict orders against any of us recruiting our own bed partners at the point of a gun."

Captain Gringo said, "He sounds like a swell guy. Who is he and how did he get to be a general?"

Royce said, "Oh, we're nominally under the command of a General Ramos. A Spic, of course, but not a bad sort, really. He was appointed by the Cuban Government in Exile to lead this expeditionary force. Doesn't seem to know his arse from his elbow. No Spics know a thing about military tactics. But he doesn't get in the way much. Once in a while one of us real soldiers has to tell him which end of a gun the round comes out of, but he's an agreeable old fart and takes suggestions well."

"I see. Who suggested the bit about the local girls serving as our play pretties whether they wanted to or not?"

Royce frowned thoughtfully and replied, "I really can't say. One of us must have. Are you some sort of greaser-lover, Walker?"

"Depends on what they look like. I'm not out to fight any windmills, Major. Uncle Sam once sentenced me to death for trying to right what I thought was an injustice. I just like to know *why*, when natives start swinging machetes at my dome. I take it this Cuba Libre force is provisioned the same way it gets its quarters and quiff?''

"Of course. The homeowners required to quarter our troops are naturally supposed to feed them as best they can. But if they run short the General's standing orders are that the neighbors just have to supply the extra provisions. It's no problem, look you. Almost every peon in town keeps pigs and chickens if not a goat or milk cow."

They were already coming to the end of the main drag, Progreso not being a large town. As they were passing a cactus hedge a skinny little Mexican with Mayan features and a machete in his hand popped out of a gap in the nopales, screaming something about his daughter, his pig, or both. Before he'd gotten to the point, or come anywhere near anyone with that wildly swinging machete, Royce had calmly pointed his twelve-gauge and blown the man almost in two with a double blast of number nine buck. As the Mexican beat his fluttering sombrero to the dust and just lay there, Royce said, "See what I mean? Some of them act crazy even when they can *see* you're armed, look you!"

Captain Gringo stared down at the pathetic corpse in the spreading pool of blood and guts without comment. In fairness to Royce, he didn't see what else the Welshman could have done. But he was beginning to understand the dead man's point of view, too. Royce said, "Let's go, shall we?" as he stepped over the man he'd shot, reloading his shotgun as he did so. Captain Gringo and Gaston walked around the gory mess. Neither asked Royce who was supposed to clean up after him. They knew.

Royce led them around the next corner, down the block of walled inwardly facing houses a ways, then stopped at a substantial oaken door, saying, "Ah, here we are."

The Welshman knocked on the door with the muzzle of his shotgun. Naturally it opened without keeping them waiting long. A small, dark, frightened-looking chica seemed to be trying not to cry as she murmured, "Estrada, por favor. I shall take you to La Señora."

She did, or at least she led Captain Gringo across the pateo to the main salon of the establishment as Royce turned away to go back to wherever he wanted to. The maid vanished too, once she'd presented them to a not bad but stern-looking white woman pretending to be Queen Victoria on her thronelike seat by the cold hearth of her baronial fireplace.

She sniffed and said in English, "So you're the two gun-thugs General Ramos has seen fit to shove down my throat, eh? Very well. Behave yourselves and I won't poison you. Lucrecia will show you to the quarters we've prepared for you and you'll find your engines of destruction waiting for you there. The rascals who brought it in tracked mud all over my floors, and I'll thank you to remember this is a respectable house! I dine at eight sharp, every evening. You two will be fed at six, by my servant, in the kitchen. You are free to come and go as you like, of course, since I have nothing to say about your no doubt marvelous military plans. But I'll thank you to stay out of my back garth. There is nothing of interest to you there and some of my, ah, livestock bites!"

Captain Gringo decided he liked her. He smiled and said, "We won't give you any trouble, Miss . . . ah?"

"Prunella Parsons," she snapped, adding, "*Doctor* Prunella Parsons, Biology. Biology is the study of Life, a subject few professional soldiers would be interested in. Your own officers have already searched my biological specimens for hidden weapons and assured themselves I am a harmless eccentric. I only wish I could be as sure about *you* two. Don't either of you ever *shave*, for heaven's sake?"

Captain Gringo sheepishly fingered his shipboard stubble and said, "We weren't expecting to meet a lady so soon, Miss Prunella. If you'd have your servants show us to our quarters we'll get right to making ourselves more presentable.''

She said, "I doubt that. I only have one servant and she's frightened half to death. I've assured her she's safe. I hope neither of you will make a liar out of me.''

She clapped her hands, and when the nervous Lucrecia tiptoed back in, told the chica in perfect Spanish to get these louts out of her sight. So they followed the Mexican girl, although Gaston could not resist telling their reluctant hostess what he thought of her in a Berber dialect he'd picked up serving with the Legion in Algeria.

For the first time since they'd met her, Prunella Parsons smiled, and replied in the same language, but more fluently, "You're not man enough, oh son of a sway-backed camel and a hunch-backed jinn.''

Gaston laughed incredulously and told her, "Eh bien, I had that coming to me. Mais you certainly don't *look* Saharan, m'selle.''

She shrugged and said, "My work takes me lots of places, and *your* place is still *upstairs*, effendi.''

That was where Lucrecia took them. As she led them along the corridor, Gaston chuckled and said, "I like her. She's almost old enough for me, too. Remember I saw her first, Dick.''

Captain Gringo laughed and said, "She's all yours, but I doubt it. I admire the old dame's spunk, too. But if a guerrilla army can't make her really knuckle under, she shapes up as a pretty hard conquest for any man, don't you think?''

"Poof, I have always enjoyed a challenge. The poor child has been an obvious virgin long enough. So stand back and let your elders show you how the path to a maiden's cherry orchard may be won!''

The mental picture was so amusing Captain Gringo laughed again, louder. The little Mexican girl had no idea what they were talking about in English, but it made her nervous anyway. Women can always tell when men are laughing lewdly about something, and as far as she could tell she was the only thing in a skirt anywhere near them. So they were obviously laughing that way about her, and by the time they came to Gaston's door Lucrecia was blushing furiously.

Gaston approved the spacious clean layout and said so graciously in Spanish. In the same language Captain Gringo said, "This is very nice. Now suppose you show me what you have for *me*, Lucrecia."

She gulped, ducked around him, and motioned for him to follow. As they passed another door he asked why that wasn't it and she explained, "That is La Señora's laboratorio, for to cut up animals and mix strange potions. She keeps the door locked and I am never to go in there. Do you think it is true what people say about her. señor?"

"What do they say, Lucrecia?"

"That she may be a bruja. She has been very kind to me, but some brujas deal in white magic, too, no?"

He chuckled and said, "I don't think she's a witch, Lucrecia. In our country, what she does is called experimentad, see?"

"I think so, this experimentad is some kind of white Yanqui magic?"

"Close enough. I promise she won't turn you into a frog."

Lucrecia looked a bit relieved, but not very, as she opened the door beyond and said, "This is where La Señora said to put you and all those boxes, señor."

She followed him in as he entered what could have passed for a fairly posh guest room if the big brass bedstead and other furniture hadn't been forced to share the limited space with a pile of raw pine crates. Most of them were stenciled, "Woodbine Arms Limited, .30-30 Ball. Webbed." But a larger, longer crate atop the ammo had been stenciled, "Maxim Patent Machine Gun. .30-30. One. Tripod Mount. One. Tool Kit. One."

He moved over to the pile, saw everthing was nailed

tightly and that the Maxim crate was oozing heavy grease. He grimaced and said, "Hell with it. I've plenty of time and maybe La Señora has a crow bar in her tool shed. I don't feel up to it right now, and how much more can it rust in one afternoon?"

He'd been speaking mostly to himself, of course. So he was mildly surprised, when he turned away, to see Lucrecia was still there and that she'd shut and barred the door. He was more surprised that she was on the bed, silently weeping with her little brown hands to her face. He moved over to the bed, sat down beside her, and put an arm around her shoulders to comfort her as she started bawling louder and he said, "Hey, hey, what's with the waterworks? You seem to be scared skinny, querida!"

She sobbed, "Si, I am. I have never done this before and you are so big, even though you are nice looking."

He frowned and asked, "What have I got to do with whatever you're so upset about? What is it you're supposed to do that you've never done before and obviously don't want to?"

She sniffled and explained, "La Señora says I am pretty. So it is only a question of time before one of you soldados wishes for to fuck me. She says it would be smarter for me to give myself to one officer and save myself from being passed around from soldado to soldado. So when we heard two officers were to be staying here, she said I was to pick one and . . . you know. But now that I have picked you, I am still, as you say, scared skinny!"

He nodded soberly and said, "Look, it happens. Some girls just manage somehow to stay virgins. But stop bawling about it, damn it."

She flinched at the slight annoyance in his tone and pleaded, "Do not beat me. por favor! I will do anything you say, if only you will be . . .gentle. But you shall have to show me what it is you want of me. For alas, I know nothing of such matters."

He smiled wistfully and said, "I never would have

guessed. Look, Lucrecia, it's all right. You have nothing to worry about. I'm not going to trifle with you, see?''

''Es verdad? You do not wish for me to take my clothes off now?''

''Not hardly. I'm not *that* much of a gentleman. I like my olives green, but I don't like climbing trees to get at them. So dry your tears and go wash some dishes or something. I'd say I was sorry I scared you, if it had been my idea. But the war is over, so let's just forget about it.''

She peered up at him curiously between her forked tear-soaked fingers and asked, ''What am I to tell La Señora? That you simply found me too ugly?''

He laughed and told her, ''Tell her anything you like. But let's not play games, kitten. I said I wouldn't mess with you if you didn't want me to. I never said I was a sissy!''

''I do not understand, señor.''

''I know. Sometimes I have trouble understanding me, too. If you don't want to get laid, get lost. Is that plain enough for you?''

She sobbed. ''I know I should be practical, as La Señora calls it, but I am just too frightened. Are you angry with me?''

''Not yet. But I'll never forgive myself, either way, if you don't get out of here, poco tiempo.''

So she rose and ran sobbing to unbar the door, dash out, and slam it shut behind her. Captain Gringo swore softly and muttered, ''All right, so we do feel up to inspecting that fucking Maxim after all. Right now I could probably pry the crate open with this hard-on and it's better, at times like this, for a man to have something less silly to do with his hands!''

He rose and then, knowing how most guns were shipped in the tropics, peeled off his clothes before even thinking about opening the top crate. He placed his .38 on a nearby dresser, unfolded the screwdriver blade of his pocket knife, and got to work on the nails. He pried a board off, muttered, "Aw, shit," and paused to light a claro while his hands were still greaseless. Then he dug into the packing and started hauling shit out. He tried to make sure most of the greasy sawdust fell back in the crate, but a lot of it wound up on the floor anyway. There was no carpeting to worry about and sweeping the shit up would probably do the unpainted floor planks some good, too, so what the hell.

He got the tool kit out first, wiped the waterproofed canvas as clean as he could with his now greasy hands, and spread the tools out on the dresser by his .38. The fucking tripod could stay where it was for now. What could go wrong in transit with a tripod, even if he ever meant to use the silly thing?

The machine gun itself was the matter before the house. The water jacket was empty, of course, but the heavy weapon still thunked pretty solid across the crate edges. He took the water jacket off first and leaned it against the wall. Then he cranked open the action, stared morosely down at the buttery goo filling the breech, and muttered, "What am I doing? I need rags, lots of rags, just to see what the fuck I'm doing!"

He wiped some of the grease from his palms to his chest, took a towel from the rack above the corner washstand, and wrapped it around his middle. Then he picked up the .38 and went outside to call for Lucrecia. She came up the stairwell, took one look at him, and sobbed, "Oh my God! You do not need a *gun*, señor! I *said* I would not fight back!"

He laughed and said, "I need rags, a lot of rags. Cotton, if you can manage. The gear they gave me to clean is messier than I expected."

She looked and vanished after saying she'd be right back. He returned to his chore, knotting the towel around his middle as he placed the .38 back on the dresser, took a deep drag on his cigar, and gingerly stuck a finger in the goo to feel if anything was broken enough to notice the

easy way. The bolt seemed okay and, yeah, the firing pin
was in place, but . . . where in the hell was the arming rod?

When Lucrecia came in with an armful of cotton rags
Captain Gringo was cursing like a pirate's parrot as he
disassembled the damned gun and covered himself with
grease at the same time. The young peon girl was more
upset by the fact the towel had slipped from around his
waist and lay on the floor at his feet. He was too steamed
to have an erection, but that part of him was covered with
thick brown goo, too. He snapped, "Get over here with
those rags. Pile them on the windowsill here, and hand me
a big one, pronto!"

She did as she was told, starting to cry again. He was
too worried about more important matters to notice or to
care if he had. He got to work with the rag, wiping parts
clean as he stripped them and put them aside. Lucrecia
didn't know what else he wanted, so she sat on the bed
again to wait and see. She knew she shouldn't be looking
where she was looking, but she'd never seen anything like
that before. It was much bigger than she'd been led to
expect and . . . was it *possible* some women not only managed to accomodate such a monstrous male organ but
even, in fact, enjoy it, as some boasted? As the big man
turned to place the bolt on the dresser he saw she was
looking at him and she quickly asked, "Is there anything I
can do for to help?"

He started to say no. Then he said, "Yes, if you hold
one end of the barrel steady it night be easier to unscrew
from the block. My hands are slippery and I can't get a
purchase on this damned stripped screw head!"

She didn't know what he was talking about. But she was
willing to learn. As she gingerly took hold of the muzzle
for him Lucrecia wrinkled her pert little nose and said,
"Oh, it's so *messy,* señor!"

He said, "I know. Why don't you slip out of your skirt
and blouse? That way you won't get them grease stained."

He'd assumed she had a slip on under her outer garments.

She just assumed she was supposed to do as she was told. So when she did as he asked and wound up shyly holding the other end of the gun barrel stark naked, he nodded and said, "Right. I think you'd better call me Dick from here on, Lucrecia. Señor sounds a little formal, considering. Can't you hold that any tighter? I can't unscrew it if you let it twist in your hands like that."

The petite brown-skinned peon frowned with determination, bent her knees, and gripped the barrel as tightly as she could by locking it between her upper arm and torso as well as her tight little fists. Her left tit sure tooked cute, perched on the gun barrel like that. And, better yet, it worked. The reluctant screw yielded with a sudden pop and he said, "Bueno. You can let go now."

She did, wiping at her greasy torso with greasy hands and of course only getting herself greasier. She said, "Oh, how am I to ever put my blouse back on now?" and he said, "Don't worry. We've still got plenty of clean cotton rags and there's soap and water as well up here. Let's see if some idiot put the rod I'm looking for up the goddamn barrel. It has to be *someplace*, right?"

She swore she didn't have whatever he was looking for. He said he could see that. Then he held the barrel like a spy glass, sighed, and said, "Oh, the stupid mother-fucking sons of bitches!"

Lucrecia cowered away, covering her greasy little breasts with her hands as she pleaded, "Please don't be angry, Deek!"

He put the barrel down, saying, "Hey, hey, sorry. I wasn't fussing at *you*. I was fussing at whoever assembled this Maxim without an arming rod."

"Is that a wicked thing for to do, Deek?"

"It's worse than wicked. Without an arming rod a machine gun won't work. A machine gun that won't work can be an awful thing to fight with and they say Los Rurales may pay us a visit before we can get to pay the Bay of Pigs a visit."

She gasped, "Los Rurales? Oh, no! Save me! Save me!
I know what Los Rurales do, even to ugly women and, if
they can't get an ugly woman, pretty boys!"

Every pretty girl in Mexico knew about Los Rurales and
Lucrecia was prettier than most. So without thinking she'd
dashed over to throw her greasy naked body in Captain
Gringo's greasy arms. His greasy dong, upon finding itself
pressed against naked female flesh, began to act as greasy
dongs often do on such occasions, whether anyone asks
them to or not. As he held Lucrecia against him to comfort
her trembling little trembling parts he raised his eyes
heavenward and muttered, "Look, God, I tried, but enough
is enough!"

He picked her up and carried her over to the bed. They
were going to make an awful mess, but the old dame
downstairs had told the girl to seduce him and was it her
fault he wasn't neat?

As he lowered her to the counterpane, Lucrecia said,
"Oh you are so strong, Deek. But I do not think I am big
enough for you, even if I knew how!"

He reclined beside her, close, and began to spread the
grease evenly over her brown flesh as he soothed, "Let me
be the judge of that. Take it easy, I won't hurt you. We'll
make all the stops on the way there and, hmm, this stuff
sure is slippery, isn't it?"

"It feels . . . stimulating. Nobody ever told me men rub
axle grease all over women, Deek."

"They don't, all over, as a rule. Let me show you where
a little lubrication might be just the ticket for a sweet little
thing like you."

He bent to kiss her as he slid her free hand from her
axle-greased left nipple down her belly and beyond, to
where it would do them both more good. She couldn't say
anything with him kissing her, which was the general idea,
but she flinched and tried to cross her thighs on his
grease-slicked hand as he cupped her mons and began to
grease her love engine with two fingers, rocking her

aroused clit in the boat as he did so. When she suddenly moaned and began to move her hips in time with his petting he lifted his lips from hers and said, "See? Nothing to it. Does that hurt, querida?"

"Oh, no, it feels glorioso! But please don't rape me, Deek. I am still afraid, a little, I think."

He said, "They don't call this rape. It's called seduction, see?"

"Oh? What is the difference between rape and seduction, Deek?"

"Salemanship. Could you move your thighs apart a little farther?"

"Like this? Oh, what are you *doing* to me, Deek?"

He didn't recall the Spanish for finger fucking, so he just kept doing it as he soothed, "Just getting you greased right, where it matters. Hey, look, I can get three fingers in now. Does it hurt?"

"Not really, but it feels so strange, now. Maybe you had better stop. Oh, oh, if you do not take your hand away from there I fear I am about to pee pee on it! I am trying not to, but I have no control now and, oh, oh, ohhhhhhhhhhhhh!"

He went on petting her gently as her postorgasmic contractions subsided. He said nothing. There were times when a guy could blow it by saying the wrong thing to a bewildered woman and this one had to be mixed up as hell about now. She was. She heaved a vast sigh and asked, "What happened, just now? That most certainly did not feel at all like pissing, even if it was with the same muscles."

He kissed her again and murmured, "I think you just came. Did you like it?"

"I don't know. I think so. But it felt so strange I was frightened at the same time. Maybe if we tried it again . . ."

He rolled atop her before she could change her mind. She tried to as she felt him positioning himself to enter her properly, or, as she might have still thought, most improperly. She said, "Wait, not that way! With your fingers some more! I don't want that awful thing in me! It's too big! It's all covered with axle grease! It's...Oh, my God, it's *inside* me and if you don't take it out, deeper, deeper, yesssss!''

So that was how Lucrecia lost her virginity, although, as she later coyly put it, virginity was nothing to lose if it meant gaining such a nice friend. They spent the whole siesta furthering her education and by the time she said, with a sigh, she had to go downstairs and began to prepare supper, she'd become an enthusiastic as well as experienced lover. For though some guys were too shy to advance beyond the missionary position through an entire honeymoon, Captain Gringo didn't see fit to fool around. When a man lived on the run and might never see a pretty girl again, he got all he could out of experience he could. The grease helped a lot. But as she bathed and dressed he told her they'd try something cleaner, or at least neater, later that night. Lucrecia said she could hardly wait.

When she'd left, he wiped himself as clean as he could on dry cotton, then took a whore bath to get the rest off. He pulled the soiled counterpane off the bed and lay naked on the cleaner linen below. He'd just had a great lay, he had plenty of smokes, and it soon would be time to eat. If Lucrecia cooked half as well as she screwed he was looking forward to it. So why was he still muttering curses? He was trying to figure out how one got a machine gun to fire full automatic without an arming rod

There wasn't any. Without the missing part to rearm the chamber automatically after each shot, a Maxim could only be fired like a repeating rifle by pulling the arming lever back by hand for each shot, and who wanted a gun that fired like a bolt-action Krag but weighed as much as a dozen of the same?

He knew what the missing part looked like. He knew how to make one, given the right tools and materials. There was probably a machine shop somewhere in this dinky seaport. A turret lathe would be too much to ask for, but with steamers putting in here fairly regularly some boat yard ought to have at least a screw-cutting lathe and Inshallah, a steel-cutting power saw. The *steel* was going to be the problem. Old Hiram Maxim hadn't designed his machine gun with mild steel in mind. The vital part missing took one hell of a beating. He'd broken rods made by the factory firing a little more frantic than the Maxim was designed to take. Nothing he was going to find in the stock of a local herrera figured to be good for making anything but fancy wrought-iron grille-work. Machine steel some ship's chandler might have on tap figured to be too heavy gauge. One needed no-kidding hunks of alloy steel to put steamship gear back together and the Maxim was hardly a steam engine. But maybe a local clocksmith . . . Forget it, a heavy machine gun wasn't a grandfather clock, either! The missing part required stock somewhere between the delicate innards of a clock and the massive machinery of a steamboat. There was nothing he could do about it this late in the day. So he told himself to forget it for now. It was easy, like trying to forget about a mosquito in one's bedroom at night, except that bullets stung somewhat harder and, damn it, they were going to need that goddamn Maxim before this show was over!

Meanwhile, not having Lucrecia in his own room as a lovely distraction, Gaston had gotten bored and gone exploring on his own. He'd been about to knock on Captain Gringo's door for company when he heard the younger couple talking inside and discreetly chuckled away with out disturbing them, Downstairs, he'd found nobody about. So he poured himself a healthy snort at the corner bar their missing hostess surely intended to be used and strolled out to the kitchen with it, to see what they were having for supper.

But since the only cook on the premises was upstairs,

about to have Captain Gringo any time now, there was nothing interesting going on in the kitchen. Gaston helped himself to some red peppers hanging by the stove and wandered out the back door, drink in one hand as he nibbled peppers from the other. Unlike the pateo out front, Prunella Parsons had indeed turned her rear enclosure into a combination of kitchen garth and . . .zoo? Cages lined the stucco walls around three sides of the enclosure. The prim Doctor Parsons was at the moment standing before one of them with her back to Gaston as he strolled toward her. She'd changed to a shapeless smock of light tan whipcord and was holding a riding crop in her hands behind her as she crooned, "That's it, Tigre. Good Tigre, nice Tigre, be nice to the pretty goat, Tigre."

Gaston moved closer, looked beyond her, and saw that in the cage a large male jaguar was fornicating with a smaller black nanny goat. The jaguar seemed to be enjoying it. The goat had nothing to say about it. She'd been tied between two stakes with her no-doubt in heat as well as confused rear end exposed to the big cat's lust. The jaguar was apparently a little confused about its unusual sex partner, too. For it suddenly dismounted and moved over to sit in a corner of the cage, licking its big pink erection. Prunella stamped her foot and snapped, "Damn, you men are all alike!"

Gaston decided to back away quietly. But before he could ease back to the kitchen door Prunella had lowered a barred slide between the jaguar and its bleating lover, victim, or whatever, and turned around. She gasped when she saw Gaston standing there. The dapper little Frenchman nodded pleasantly and said, "Bon après-midi, m'selle. A lovely afternoon for a stroll in the garden, non?"

"Damn it, it's siesta time. I thought nobody would be about."

"A reasonable assumption, I am sure. But do not let me disturb you. I shall be in the main salon should you need me, or should that très attractive nanny need a new partner.''

She laughed despite herself and said, ''Wait. I'd better explain. What you just saw was a scientific experiment, not perversion on my part, if that's what you were thinking.''

Gaston smiled politely and asked, ''Why should such a thought have crossed my mind? It was not *you* in the cage just now, hein? As a matter of fact I did once meet a woman who made love to her pet jaguar. Her whole family was très nuts, too. It did not work out so well. The could never have children, and I suspect in the end it ate her. In the literal rather than romantique sense, I mean.''

''Oh, my God, I hope you're just joshing!''

''Mais non, I never joke about my favorite subject, sex. As for bestiality, there may be times and places when being an animal lover, with enthusiasm, is the lesser of two evils. I'm sure you saw what we Legionaires were expected to sleep with in North Africa, if you were there long enough to learn Berber, but alas the camels were as ugly and the Bedu guarded their sheep more carefully than the did their daughters, so I know little of the subject.''

He turned to go back to the house. She fell in step beside him and said, ''You're a terrible man and I'm not sure *I'd* trust you with a sheep, either! But I still want to explain. As you know, goats are usually killed as prey by jaguars.''

''Oui, obviously that one was not hungry just now. Training jungle cats to make love to livestock instead of eating it shows some promise, but frankly I don't think it's a practique solution to the problem.''

''Heavens, that's not why I'm trying to teach Tigre to mate with his usual prey. It's an experiment in instinctual modification. You see, unlike our own somewhat imaginative species, it never occurs to lower animals, under ordinary circumstances, to mate with anything but their own kind.''

''Eh bien, any farm boy can tell you that. Pigs have to

be persuaded with considerable force, even when the farm boy is good looking."

By this time they were back inside. So Prunella asked if he'd like his glass freshened as she built herself her own heroic highball. He held out his glass and she freshened it indeed, with straight white rum. He noticed she didn't use much mixer, either. She led him over to the sofa. They sat down and she said, "As I was saying, left to themselves, lower animals don't, well, commit bestiality, if we define bestiality as two creatures of opposite sex but different species . . . ah . . . "

"Fucking is the word in English, non?"

She almost spilled her drink but recovered her calm, if now less severe, expression. He liked the way she'd let her hair down, too. Her soft salt and pepper waves framed her aristocratic if somewhat over-the-hill bone structure nicely. She said, "Very well, as long as you remember this is a scientific discussion, fucking is the most sensible word for it. Knowing how some people feel about the subject, more so here in a Catholic country where bestiality's unheard of—"

"You are wrong," Gaston cut in flatly, adding, "If the practice was not so common, the church would not have made so many très fatigué rules against it. You forget Mexico is mostly a rural society. A boy, or, merde, a girl who watches animals breeding all the time and never feels any curious stirrings is, at best, très unimaginative, and if they then find nothing better to do about it but play with themselves—another vile sin according to the church— they are stupid as well, non?"

"Oh, Gaston, what are you saying?"

"That any farm boy who says he has never at least tried it with a très friendly pet in heat is a liar, of course."

"You seem to know a lot about the subject. Have you ever . . . ?"

"I am a city boy. Besides, I never kiss and tell. However, speaking as a city boy who once worked in a très exclusive Paris hotel, I can tell you it's an accepted fact, in hotel circles, that any chic woman of the world, traveling alone with a brace of large dogs, say Russian wolfhounds, is always very fond of them. It is the *two male* dogs that gives the show away. From my observations at peepholes meant to catch more sinister crimes in progress, one observes one dog, alone, is not enough to satisfy the human female appetite. Dogs are worse than men when it comes to simply stopping once they come.''

She blushed deeply and said, ''I'm not sure this scientific conversation is as clinical as it should be. I know domestic pets can be trained to do almost anything for their masters. That is, I mean I've read the literature on the subject. I didn't mean I knew . . . Oh, dear, I *knew* nobody else would understand my work!''

Gaston sipped his drink, shrugged, and said, ''I do not find it difficult to understand, m'selle. Everyone is très curious about sex. I once paid ten pesos to watch a double-jointed homosexual, or perhaps autosexual is the better term, do something très disgusting to himself on a cantina bar. I assure you I felt no desire to *join* him there!'' He took another sip, chuckled to himself, and added, ''Mais of course, once I got home, and nobody was looking . . . But getting back to your *own* scientific interests, ah, Prunella mon petite, would it help you stop blushing if I confessed I have, on a very few occasions, made the zig zig with a friendly creature who although unable to tell me how much it liked it, nevertheless seemed to enjoy the novelty, too?''

''My God, how could you confess such a thing to a strange woman?''

''If you'd ever seen my first wife, you'd agree a llama is prettier. I did not say I made a regular *habit* of the vile practice. I have never worked as a sheep herder. By the way, did you know sheep *dogs* do it, too? There's an example of a beast of prey and an herbivore mating willingly, non? Of course, canines are more lusty than felines. Perhaps if you let your jaguar at that goat in the dark—''

''I tried that. It ate the goat,'' she cut in, adding with a sigh, ''I know big cats are driven more by instinct than dogs. I have a Great Dane out back who seems willing to mate with goats, pigs, tapirs, even ... never mind. I'm interested in species that, as you say, are more driven by instinct.''

''I knew a girl one time who had a pet rabbit that kept fucking her cat every time it was in heat. We used to watch. Fifi said it made her très hot to watch. Does it excite you sexually to watch other creatures fucking, Prunella?''

''Of course not. I'm a scientist, not a sex maniac,'' she protested. Then she drained her glass, put it down, and pulled Gaston up after her, saying, ''Let's go up to my lab. I want to show you something.'' He went with her, resisting the impulse to ask if she had bed bugs indulging in sex with spiders under glass. The conversation had stimulated him a bit as well, and for a woman her age Prunella's derrière certainly moved nicely under that thin smock. He wondered what she had on under it.

Prunella Parsons had nothing on under her smock. As soon as she had Gaston alone behind a locked door she peeled it off, exposing a surprisingly youthful figure, when one considered how gray her hair was, all over. Gaston naturally reached for his own buttons as he asked to what he owed this great honor.

She said, ''I've been looking for someone like you to help me in my work. I've only one pair of hands and the creatures can be so stubborn ... But let's talk about it later, after we get this silly sexual tension between us out of the way!''

So Gaston took her in his own naked arms, lowered her to the lab's convenient leather chesterfield, and put his naked virile member right where they both wanted it. As he entered her, Prunella gasped, "Jesus! You seem to be a lot taller than you look!"

"Merci. How would you say I stack up, say next to your jaguar? I never got to ask that other girl."

She laughed as she wrapped her long legs around his skinny hips and began to bump and grind, saying, "I wouldn't know yet. I've been afraid to try, although that certainly would be a test of, ah, instinct versus conditioning. But now that I have you to help me, if you're really as understanding as you say, would you, could you, after everyone else is in bed tonight, come out to the cages with me?"

He kissed her gallantly and said, "Why not, if I get to fuck the pretty nanny goat as well?"

Despite the sudden thaw, their hostess got to dine alone at eight that evening anyway, whether she wanted to or not, because a messenger arrived at five, or just about the time the soldiers of fortune were putting their pants back on, to tell them General Ramos was ready to see them now. So they told their new girlfriends to be faithful till they got back and followed the mestizo messenger back toward the main plaza. He was the first member of the Cuba Libre invasion force they'd seen that looked anything like a Cuban. But when Gaston commented on this, the darker-skinned hombre explained that like them he was simply a soldier of fortune, in his case from Panama. They didn't ask him much more. He obviously had no idea what was going on around here either.

General Ramos received them graciously on the veranda of the house he'd taken over from its original Mexican owners. The General was a portly middle-aged Creole seated in a big peacock chair of wickerwork. He was wearing a uniform that would have looked gaudy on a hotel doorman back in the States. The dame seated next to him in a less imposing chair was pretty spectacular, too. The General introduced her as his adelita, Señorita Vegas y Montez. She smiled graciously enough, but she looked as if she thought her shit didn't stink.

Other than that, the view down the front of her low-cut gown wasn't bad. Like the General she was almost pure white, albeit that rather pleasing shade of peach girls seemed to come in in the south of Spain. The general indicated comfortable enough but much more humble wicker chairs across the low coffee table he and his mistress were enthroned behind. There was nothing on it to eat or drink. Captain Gringo and Gaston sat down anyway.

General Ramos said, "Bueno. I like to get to know my officers a few at a time, in private man-to-man conversations. Naturally I know all about you two. Your records are most impressive. So I would like you to tell me, frankly, what you think of my army, so far."

For once Gaston had nothing to say. He seemed more interested in the yummy-looking dame across the table from them. So Captain Gringo said, "We haven't seen very much of an army, yet, sir. But I do have a problem with the Maxim you issued me. It won't shoot."

"Es verdad? Surely you can fix it, no? You were an ordinance officer in the U.S. Army before your, ah, misunderstanding with your superior, right?"

"I know how to repair weapons, sir. But not without spare parts. My machine gun's not broken. They shipped it missing its arming rod. Perhaps one of the other heavy weapons sections has a spare."

"What other heavy weapons section?" The general asked, adding, "You were issued the only machine gun that's arrived so far, and if it won't work..."

"We're in trouble." Captain Gringo nodded. The he frowned and said, "They told us you planned a full-scale landing at the Bay of Pigs, sir. No offense, but one machine gun doth not a full-scale anything make, even when it's in shape to fire! Back home the current wisdom holds there should be at least two automatic weapons to cover every battalion front. If it was up to me there'd be two to a company.''

General Ramos brushed a fly from his face and said, ''You are not back home. The Spanish defenders probably won't have *any* machine guns, and in any case we shall surely have a few more arriving any time now. In God's truth our, ah, backers have been a bit slow in delivering the supplies they promised us. But it is no problem. Until I have this army of liberation up to full strength I do not intend to budge from here. Have you any other comments to make, Captain Gringo?''

The tall American knew better. But what the hell, the slob had asked, so he nodded and said, ''Yessir. As I said, we haven't seen much yet. But I couldn't help getting the impression you have an awful lot of chiefs and I don't see any Indians.''

The general frowned and said he didn't understand. Captain Gringo could see that. But he still said, ''You've recruited soldiers of fortune from all over Latin America. Most of us have taken up the trade because we have technical skills your average native soldado doesn't have. So the guys like us will expect to serve as officers or at the very least noncommissioned technical sergeants. None of us seem to be drawing a private's pay.''

''That is true. But make your point, Captain Gringo.''

''Isn't it obvious, sir? For every corporal in every army, and you're not about to get a soldier of fortune to serve as a corporal, there's supposed to be a corporal's squad of at least eight privates. Every second lieutenant is supposed to lead at least a twenty-four-man platoon, and every captain a minimum of seventy-two combat soldiers along with his orderly room staff and so forth.''

''I know all that, son. Hell, I am a *general*!''

''I was sure you'd have heard it somewhere, General.

So, okay, where are the troops to follow all us officers and senior NCOs?''

Ramos looked pained and explained, ''We have been experiencing some difficulty in recruiting common soldados. Governor Weyler's harsh methods have apparently impressed the lower-class Cubanos with less to gain and little understanding of politics. To even spell Libertad one must know how to read and write, no? But do not worry, once we establish our beachhead and run up the new Cuban banner, no doubt the local populace will rally to our cause and we can arm all the common soldiers we need on the spot.''

That was too stupid to even argue about. So Captain Gringo shurgged and said, ''Let's talk about here and now, then, sir. I couldn't help but notice your recruits here on the mainland have been a little high-handed as far as the *local* populace goes. If you're not planning on leaving soon, like say tonight, it might be a good idea to ease up on the Mexican townspeople. They'd see little point in a Cuban occupation even if they could be sure their chickens, pigs and women were going to be treated with respect and . . .'' But the general cut him short with a weary wave of his hand and said, ''You do not have to tell me some of the roughnecks we've recruited have been acting rough, Captain Gringo. I have done my utmost to make them behave like gentlemen. But this is war, and in wartime such things must be expected, no?''

''Maybe, General. But Mexico hasn't declared war on anybody and, just between us girls, Mexicans are tough fighting men when you push them into it. I try not to. The ones here in Yucatan are mostly pure Indian with a thin veneer of Spanish Catholic culture. That can be a pretty explosive mixture.''

General Ramos chuckled and asked, ''Are you trying to explain the customs of Spanish Catholics to *me*, Captain *Gringo?*

''Somebody has to, sir. You hidalgos of pure Spanish blood seem to have more trouble understanding your campesinos than Texans, and you should see Laredo on a Saturday night! Spaniards, like Anglos, are Europeans at heart. So despite the flamenco singing and other somewhat different notions, you share the white European's caste system and serene indifference to what the servants are talking about in the kitchen. Knocking around down here as a guerrilla leader I've gotten to look behind the scenery. So I feel free to tell you half the comic opera revolutions could be avoided if the ruling classes bothered to consider the feelings of the ruled.''

General Ramos frowned and said, ''They never told us you were a follower of that strange German Jew, Karl Marx!''

Captain Gringo shook his head and said, ''I'm not. I've read his so-called manifesto and I think *he's* never talked to his servants either. I'm not accusing your class of deliberate wrong-doing, sir. I know many a paternalistic Hispanic landlord treats his people a lot nicer than some of the guys running cotton mills or coal mines back where I come from. I just wish someone would pay attention to the fact that the rulers and the ruled down here might as well have come from different worlds. Come to think of it, they did. A handful of Europeans arrived four hundred years or so ago, licked the native rulers, and told the survivors to put on pants and show up for mass the following Sunday or else. They did, and so your kind's assumed ever since that you turned them into Spanish peasants. You didn't. You made a mess of American Indians to outwardly conform to your own idea of civilization. But they don't think like you and you don't think like them. So this afternoon a skinny guy jumped out of a cactus hedge like a wild Indian and had to be treated as one. If this was a little European town the peasants would know they just had to take a certain amount of abuse from an occupation force. They've had lots of practice in the past few thousand years. These Mexicans you're letting your guys walk over haven't. They've only been peasants a little while, and they still think a warrior's supposed to fight back when raiders from another tribe mess with their kith and kin!''

General Ramos yawned. His adelita was getting bored, too. So the General took out his watch, sighed, and said, ''This is all most interesting, Captain Gringo. But I have other officers to interview. Could we, ah, stick to practical matters? It is not my task to change the customs of unwashed Mexicans. We shall soon be off to liberate my own country and, meanwhile, we, not they, have all the guns.''

''If we could get them to shoot,'' sighed Captain Gringo.

Gaston yawned, too, but suddenly chimed in, ''We shall no doubt improvise a new arming rod for my young friend's Maxim, Mon General. I know where we can get all the iron bars we might need. Mais before we take leave of you and your enchanting companion, may I ask what the latest reports on the Mexican Rurales may happen to be?''

''Rurales? What Rurales? Nobody has said anything to me about Los Rurales.'' Ramos frowned.

Gaston said, ''No doubt they did not wish to annoy you with petty details, Mon General. But we were told, earlier, some friendly local natives reported the species lurking in the forest just outside of town.''

Ramos shrugged and decided, ''Probably just a rumor. If one could call any of the locals *friendly,* eh? Perhaps they are simply trying to encourage us to leave early.''

Gaston nodded and said, ''One could see how they might. Mais have you any patrols out, and may one assume there is at least a defense perimeter surrounding this quaint Mexican village?''

They could see by his expression the fat man hadn't even thought of either, and probably didn't want to. So Captain Gringo nodded and said, ''Right. We can see you're a busy man, General. So with your permission we'd better scout up an arming rod for my Maxim.''

Neither the General nor his adelita rose as the two soldiers of fortune got up and took their leave. Out on the calle, Captain Gringo asked Gaston, "What was that about steel bars?" and Gaston said, "Our hostess, Prunella, has a whole zoo of cages out back, avec bars of all dimensions. I am sure she could spare one for you, if I asked her nicely. She seems quite fond of me now. Mais may I make an even more practique suggestion, Dick?"

Captain Gringo shook his head and said, "I've already considered it. A run for the nearest border would be more risky than just sitting tight for now. We're over two hundred miles from British Honduras as the crow flies and we're not crows. The interior jungles of Yucatan would be a bitch to plough through even if it wasn't crawling with snakes, crocs, and probably Rurales!"

"You think they're out there, then?"

"If they're not, El Presidente Diaz just doesn't give a shit about strangers trespassing on his property and the first time *I* tired to enjoy an innocent stroll through Mexico Los Rurales arrested me in uninhabited desert country. Can you see them ignoring the occupation of a whole town's worth of Mexican taxpayers?"

"Progreso is très remote from the capital, non?"

"Nothing's that remote from a tax collector. If *we* heard about what was going on here, all the way down in Costa Rica, surely a little birdy's hopped on El Presidente's windowsill by *this* late date!"

"True, mais maybe some species of gentleman's agreement has been struck off-stage, hein? When he is not butchering women and children in the name of Democracy, Diaz is sucking the ass of Tío Sam, and anyone can see you Yankees are backing the Cuba Libre Movement, though just why escapes me. I doubt if, in the end, it will make a great deal of difference to your country whether there is a Spanish colony or another piss-pot dictatorship off Florida. Mais getting back to here and now, I doubt there are any Rurales lurking about out there in the gloomy forest, Snow White. So why don't we go look for some friendly dwarves, preferably female? We don't have to make it all the way to the border in one jump. I just want to get us out of Progreso before the whole place blows up in the General's fat face!''

Captain Gringo said he'd think about it, after he got the fucking Maxim fixed, adding, ''Whether we leave the party early or not we could still use a serious weapon if we ran into *unfriendly* dwarves in the forest, Gretel. I wasn't kidding when I tried to tell that dumb fat slob the local Indians can get pretty wild. Once you get away from the sound of church bells in Yucatan, you can run into unreconstructed Maya, remember?''

''True, but you speak a little Maya, thanks to your loving ways and that bruja who cured your fever and erection that time. At least wild tribesmen we may run into in the jungle won't be as inclined to accuse us of raping their chickens and eating their daughters as the natives here!''

''Let's get back to those steel bars. Are they no-shit machine-steel or just cold-rolled low-carbon?''

''Merde alors, how should I know? I was simply watching the animals, not running chemical tests on their cages! Prunella has a chemistry set as well as a très confortable chesterfield in her lab. Would that help?''

Captain Gringo shook his head and said, ''I'm not an industrial chemist, either. I've got to take my spare parts on faith. What I'm looking for is a length of good spring steel, about as thick as a pencil, say eighteen inches long or longer. I can always cut it down after I experiment with cutting threads at each end. But I can't stretch a too-short rod, see?''

''It sounds très fatigué. If only there was another Maxim, somewhere in camp, I would be only too happy to requisition it for you by the light of the silvery moon. Mais if the idiots in charge of this lunacy knew what they were doing, I would not be so anxious to get our adorable asses *out* of here, with or without the Maxim!''

They walked on, not sure where they were going. Like

most towns in the tropics, Progreso came to life as the sun went down, which it was doing, and stayed that way until well after midnight. But the main businesses tended to be shut down after six. Mexicans wanted to *enjoy* life in the cool shades of evening, not work at it. So although the cantinas and whorehouse would be going full blast half the night, finding a hardware store open was going to be a problem.

As they approached an alley entrance, Gaston asked, "What about a steel ramrod, Dick? Surely someone in town must have an old muzzle loader left. I've yet to see an electric light here."

Captain Gringo shook his head and said, "Too skinny, not tough enough. Hold it, what's going on down the alley?"

Gaston had ears, too. So he muttered, "Dick stay out of it!" But he might as well have said it to the nearest wall. For Captain Gringo had heard a woman crying for help and was already on the way as Gaston, cursing, followed.

The girl in trouble was about fourteen, pure Maya, and backed into a doorway by a burly drunken Anglo who kept pawing and slobbering at her as she pleaded, "Por favor, señor! I am not the kind of muchacha you take me for!"

The drunken liberator of Cuba drooled, "Sure you are. You just don't know it yet. Lessee what you got under this skirt, honey lamb. For I can see you values it highly, and that means it must be good!"

A seam of her dress ripped before Captain Gringo could get to them. But when he did, it was her attacker that got damaged the most. The big Yank grabbed the ruffian by one shoulder, spun him around, and cold-cocked him with a solid right cross. The guy was big enough to stay on his feet as he staggered backward from the blow into Gaston. So Captain Gringo dropped into a fighting crouch in case he was coming back for more. But the drunk just made a funny gurgling noise deep in his throat and fell forward with a look of wonder on his face to land face down in the alley dust, eyes still open.

Captain Gringo turned to the young girl in the doorway. She was clutching at her torn blouse, but one pert little nipple was exposed anyway. She stared wildly up at the even bigger gringo and gasped, "Oh, Santa Maria! You are one of them, too!"

He smiled thinly down at her and said, "No I'm not. Would you like us to see you safely home, or would you rather do it yourself, señorita?"

She gulped and asked, "No tricks? I am free for to go?"

He nodded and she took off like a scalded cat. But halfway down the alley she turned to shout, "God bless you, señor!" before turning away to vanish in the darkness.

Captain Gringo moved closer to Gaston, stared morosely down at the figure spread out like a bear rung between them, and asked, "Why did you do that, Gaston? I could have handled him."

Gaston shrugged and said, "Oui, and then what? Do you really need more enemies, Dick? He was not too drunk to remember, once he sobered up, and who is to say how many friends he might have had that we would not know on sight, hein?"

"Okay, so you knifed him and he probably had it coming. But what do we do with him now? If the Colonel finds one of his boys dead in an alley, come morning, it could go hard on the locals in this part of town."

Gaston nodded and said, "They know that. If I know the kind of people who must live along this alley, nobody is going to find him before they've gotten rid of him. Meanwhile, may I suggest we get the fuck out of here before someone finds *us?*"

The point was well taken. They moved on just slowly enough to avoid attracting needless attention but fast enough to put some distance between them and the cadaver. They slowed down by unspoken mutual agreement once they'd swung a couple of corners. Gaston looked around and said, "Now you've done it. There are no street lamps in this working-class part of town, and I confess to being completely turned around."

Captain Gringo shrugged and replied, "What can I tell you? In a town this size, how far could the main drag be? Come on, I see a light ahead. Looks like an open shop spilling light across the walk."

It wasn't, exactly. It was even better. For as they approached the orange glow they heard the tapping of metal on metal and Captain Gringo said, "Hey, it's a herrera, open late! This could be just what we're looking for!"

"Merde alors, since when is it *we?* I just want to find my way back to the house. I promised to show Prunella some animal training tricks."

They reached the open front of the herrera. The wiry, gray-haired blacksmith glanced up from his anvil, eyed them warily, and got back to work on the wrought-iron grille he was fashioning. Other lengths of scrap iron were soaking in the coals of his forge. A young Negro was hand-pumping the blower. He was trying not to see the two strangers in the doorway, either.

Captain Gringo said, "You do fine work, señor." and the blacksmith growled, "It is a living. Do you want something, or are you simply interested in quaint native customs?"

Captain Gringo ignored the sarcasm and replied, "I have need of a rod of spring steel, about this long, about as thick as a lead pencil, or perhaps a bit thicker. I may have to machine it down in any case. Do you know of a machine shop here in Progreso, señor?"

"Over by the waterfront. I forget the name. It will be closed for the night in any case. I do not have any spring steel in any size or shape. As you can see, I am simply a shaper of peon knickknacks."

"Suppose we found a wagon spring for you to rework?

Do you think it would be possible to hammer a curved spring leaf down to a thin straight rod without losing the temper, señor?''

"No. Do I look like a swordsmith? I only know how for to work wrought iron, perhaps mild steel. It is not important whether a window grille has temper or not, if the straps are thick enough. As to hammering out steel fishing rods, you have come to the wrong place. Ask them at the machine shop in the morning. I can't help you.''

It was obvious he didn't want to, even if he could. So Captain Gringo thanked him politely and turned away. As they moved on up the calle Gaston asked why he hadn't at least asked the way back to the main drag. Captain Gringo shrugged and asked, "Do you really want to stay lost? That old guy wouldn't give a gringo the right time. Can't say I blame him. Guys on both sides can sure act like assholes.''

But then the young Negro who'd been working the blower ran after them, shouting something. They turned and the black said, "Come back, por favor, El Herrero wishes for to speak with you again!''

They exchanged glances and followed him back. The old smith had put down his hammer and produced a bottle from somewhere. Better yet, he was smiling now. He said, "My daughter just came in for some hot water. *Her* daughter, my granddaughter, is just down the calle, having some bruises attened to by the women of the neighborhood.''

"Oh, was your granddaughter hurt, señor?''

"Not as badly as she might have been, had not a pair of most simpatico cabelleros come to her rescue not long ago. Why did you not tell me who you were, señores?''

"We didn't know who we were, to you, señor.''

"That makes sense. Nobody had described you to me until just now. I am called Hector Fernandez y Vasquez. With your permission, I shall call myself your friend, for life. I am, as you see, a mere peon, but we value the honor of our women as much as anyone, and my granddaughter has always been most precious to me.''

Captain Gringo and Gaston introduces themselves to the proud old smith and after they'd shaken on it they drank on it. His pulque was the real stuff, strong and awfully hard to get down without puking. He made them take seconds before he said, ''Bueno. Tell me again about this crazy steel fishing rod you need, Captain Gringo. Could you draw it for me on paper?''

Captain Gringo could and did, using the anvil for a writing desk as he sketched the rough demension of the blank he needed on brown pattern paper. Old Hector looked it over and said, ''No problem. How soon do you need it?''

''Right about now. But mañana will do, if you're closing soon.''

''Did I say anthing about closing, muchacho? What do you take me for, a weakling who needs sleep, like a chicken? I have some stock that should work up nicely. It is, as you suggested, salvaged spring steel from one of those crazy horseless carriages. The springs did not break. The engine fell apart when someone forgot to put oil in it. I bought the remains for scrap and took it apart. I made more than my money back just by selling the wheels, for carts God meant people to use on our roads around here. Let me think, where did I store the damned springs?''

''Are you sure you can rework a leaf without losing the temper, viejo?''

''Jesus, Maria, y José, do you take me for an apprentice? I was forging steel, and tempering it, before you were born, muchacho! Your strange object will be ready before sunrise. You may pick it up any time in the morning and I swear by the beard of Santiago you shall be able for to sharpen it to a point and use if for a fencing sword if you like!''

"I thought you said you weren't a swordsmith, viejo."

"I lied. I did not know you were as a son to me, then."

It was still early. So when Gaston kept insisting he wanted to go home and pet the animals for some reason, Captain Gringo told him, "So go on, for God's sake, and pet Prunella, too, for all I care. I still want to get the lay of the land here fixed in my head, in case we have to do some broken field running in the near future. If you see Lucrecia tell her I won't be home for a while and try to stay out of her pants."

"Does she wear any?"

"No, but you know what I mean, you old goat. What was that shit about the livestock out back? Old Prunella's not enough for you?"

"If I told you you wouldn't believe me and in any case I am in a hurry to rejoin her. So adios, for now, but watch your step, Dick. You've gotten in enough trouble for one night, hein?"

They split up, Gaston heading for the house as Captain Gringo went looking for the waterfront. He found it without much effort. Unlike the more lively parts of town he passed getting there, the waterfront, between banana boats, was pretty dead at night.

A cantina was open, way down the quay, but he wasn't interested in hearing rough laughter and someone singing "La Paloma" offkey as he, she, or it strummed a guitar that needed tuning, too. He passed a ship's chandler, shut down for the night, and beyond it stood a small red brick machine shop. It was closed, too. No problem. He knew nobody below the rank of major was allowed to mess with him and it only took a few seconds to pick the simple lock. He went in and looked for a light switch. There wasn't any. Gaston had been right about them being a little out of date in Progreso. But when he struck a match and lit a handy coal oil lamp he saw the power tools were fairly new and electric powered. That prompted him to explore further and, in a back room, he found the answer. A big one-lung internal combustion engine was hooked up to a dynamo. The shop didn't bother with electric Edison bulbs, but it did have its own power source. So things were starting to look up.

He consulted his watch, shrugged, and went back outside, locking the door after him. He had to give old Hector at least a few hours before he brought the blank here to machine it down. He'd need at least the action of the Maxim to work with as well in a go no-go cut and fit to size job. So what better way to kill a few hours than with old Lucrecia, this time without the axle grease?

He chuckled as he headed back across town, softly singing the old hobo jungle ditty that went:

> "Oh the rich man uses butter,
>   The poor man uses lard,
>   The hobo uses axle grease,
>   And gets it just as hard!"

He realized the tactical error he'd made in singing in English on a dark Mexican street when at least six guys jumped him all at once, from behind, in front, and both sides!

Fortunately the Mexicans were not only less skilled in street fighting than your average knockaround guy, but there were so many of them they tended to get in each other's way, while Captain Gringo could swing at anything without worrying about hitting anyone on his side. So that's what he started doing. He decked one of them right off as, behind him, someone gasped, "Hey, that's *me* you're biting, you stupid cabrone!"

Captain Gringo reached inside his jacket for his .38 as, at the same time, he felt a healthy head of hair in the palm of the hand he was guarding with and, grabbing a big fist full of it, hung on. He could tell, as soon as he gave a healthy tug on the hair, that he was dealing with a kid or a mighty light man. So he swung the Mexican whatever off his feet and then kept him swinging in a big circle around him, knocking all sorts of people down as the one he had by the hair screamed for his mother, his father, and at least a dozen saints. Captain Gringo let go at a strategic moment, letting his victim crash into one of his few friends still on his feet, and backed into a door niche, gun drawn, as he snapped, "That's it, kids! I've got a gun and the next one gets hurt for real!"

The confused but still pissed-off gang rallied in a semi-circle around him, unwilling to either let him go or move any closer as they reconsidered their options. One said, "Hey, gringo, you really got a gun or is that a fancy lighter? Let me see it, eh? I promise for to give it back to you, amigo."

"Back off, Chico. When this thing lights up, your pals will know what it is, but *you* won't. I've got it pointed at your stupid head."

"Hey, is that any way for to talk, gringo? We just wish for to make friends with you, see? For why are you in our barrio so late at night, don't your sister want for to fuck you back home?"

Captain Grinto chuckled fondly and said, "No, I thought I'd fuck *yours*, unless she's uglier than your *mother!*"

There was a collective intake of outraged breath. The self-appointed spokesman's voice dropped to a soft thoughtful purr as he said, "I guess you know now one of us has to die, eh?"

"Be my guest, Chico. I'm betting five rounds of .38 it won't be me."

"Hey, that's not fair! When you mention an hombrés mother you owe him a mano a mano and I only got this knife!"

"Tough titty. I owe you as much as I owe a banana. They're yellow and come at a guy in bunches, too. Your mother still fucks and your father sucks. So make your move or get lost. I haven't time for kid games."

The gang did neither. They had no choice. Because suddenly a voice speaking Spanish with a Welsh accent called out, "What have we here? Don't anybody move until we find out!"

From the other side another voice snapped, "That makes it double. So's this shotgun, so make a break for it and let's see if you spics run faster than buckshot!"

Captain Gringo was feeling a lot better now than the Mexican punks, as he saw at least a dozen gun barrels trained on them from all around. He called out, "That you, Major Royce?" and the big Welshman growled, "No, it's the flaming Prince of Wales. Lucky for you we patrol a bit at night, Walker. What are you doing in this slum at this hour?"

"Took a short cut and got lost. I was just asking these guys for directions. What's with the guns?"

"What are guns usually for? Weren't these greasers trying to jump you, just now?"

"Do I look jumped? We were just kidding around. This one guy here has a rustic sense of humor, but I get along all right with the people down here."

"It didn't sound like it. Why are we speaking Spanish, by the way?"

"Wanted my pals, here, to know what we were talking about. I think you're making them nervous enough with those shotguns, Major. Could we all act a little friendlier, for God's sake? I was just messing around with some kids out looking for a good time. It's no big deal."

Royce moved closer, lowering the muzzle of his shotgun, but not much, as he said, "Right, let's get a look at your playmates."

He stared thoughtfully at the one who'd been making all the war talk and said, "Don't I know you, and didn't I kick your ass and tell you to stay in your own part of town, muchacho?"

The youth gulped and said, "I do not know who you might have kicked, señor. But this *is* my part of town! That is for why I was so happy to show this other cabellero the way back to the center, eh?"

"Is that straight, Walker?"

"Sure, why would I lie?"

Royce thought a moment, then shrugged, "You wouldn't, unless you were bonkers, look you. Let's go, lads. If this lot is harmless, that's not saying *every* greaser in town is."

Captain Gringo started to say he'd go with them. But that would have sounded dumb. So as the patrol passed out of earshot he warned the Mexicans around him, "They'll be right back if you make me fire one shot, you know."

The boy who'd been doing all the talking nodded soberly and said, "We know. It's over. But *why,* señor?"

"Do you know what they'd have done to you, all of you, if I'd said anything else?"

"Sí, that Major has killed more than one of us in the past few days. But are you not one of his men?"

"I'm a soldier of fortune, not a child molester. So if you children will just get the hell out of my way, we can forget about it."

They got the hell out of his way. He kept the gun out as he moved on up the calle, but nobody followed. One of the gang members frowned after him, muttering, "Walker? Walker? hey! You know who that was just now, Paco? It was that simpatico one! The hombre they call Captain Gringo!"

The gang leader gasped and asked, "En verdad? The one who killed all those mother-fucking Rurales down in Quintana Roo a while back?"

"It has to be him. Who else is named Walker and does not hesitate to mention a man's mother when he is outnumbered?"

Paco made the sign of the cross and said, "Madre de Dios, to think I mentioned *his* mother, too, and I am still *alive!* Vamanos, muchachos, I am buying at the cantina tonight, for I have much to celebrate! Oh, wait until I tell the girls that I, Paco Robles, am a friend of Captain Gringo himself!''

"Paco, I mean no disrespect, but would that be strictly true? Captain Gringo did not seem very friendly to any of us as he left just now."

"Don't be stupid. Of course he was being friendly. Did he shoot any of us? Did he let those others shoot us? Madre de Dios, he lied to his own kind for to save our asses. How much more friendly could a man of action be? What else would you have had him do, kiss me? I owe the big bastard my very life, and so I say he is my friend, and so I say that if any bastard in the barrio ever says one word against my pal, Captain Gringo, I, Paco Robles, will kill him and fuck all his sisters!''

Lucrecia wasn't waiting for him in his room when he let himself in back at the house. He didn't want to fall asleep. So first he went back down to the kitchen to brew himself some black coffee. Then he took the pot with him as he went exploring for some quiff to kill the main part of the night.

As he passed the upstairs doors a second time he noticed, this time, no light was coming from under Gaston's guest room, but something was up in the biology lab between. As he passed it he heard a woman sobbing incoherently. He took the coffee and cups to his own room, put them down by the bed, and went back to see who needed to be rescued this time.

He dropped to one knee and peered through the big old-fashioned keyhole. Then he bit his knuckles to keep from laughing. Their gray but remarkably well stacked hostess wasn't on the leather chesterfield Gaston had mentioned. Gaston was, naked, and old Prunella was on the floor on her hands and knees, sucking him like crazy. She was not alone down there, however. A big Great Dane he's never seen before had mounted her from behind, so Prunella was fucking and sucking at the same time, sort of. All three of them seemed to be enjoying the novel experiment in biology.

Captain Gringo found the sight a bit rich for his blood. But, damn, old Prunella sure had a great shape and Gaston, damn him, had not only gotten to her first but was wasting it on a fucking dog!

Captain Gringo grimaced and got back to his feet, muttering to himself as he went back to his own room. He felt really stupid as he undressed, because now he had a hard-on for some reason and he faced hours of time to kill with nobody to put it in. He knew if he knocked discreetly Gaston would ask him to join the orgy. But a guy had to draw the line some damned where and going sloppy seconds to a slavering beast had to be about it.

But all was not lost. For as he sat on the bed sipping coffee the door opened and Lucrecia came in, smiling shyly, as she had every right to, since she didn't have a stitch on.

She sat on the bed beside him, giggling, as he got rid of his cup in a hurry and didn't waste much time cupping one of her pretty brown breasts in one hand as he lowered her to the mattress. She said, "I heard you come in, but I was taking a bath for to make myself adorable to you."

He said she sure had as he nibbled her ear, inhaling the sweet perfume of her freshly washed hair while he ran the hand down to another nice clean place to treat it dirty. She said, "Some other officers came for to call on you earlier, querido. Your friend, Gaston, said you might not be home tonight. It made me feel so bad."

"You don't feel so bad right now. Did they say what they wanted?"

"Something about going on a patrol with you, or you

going on a patrol somewhere. I do not know much about such things. What is a patrol, Deek?''

"Trouble, if you don't do it right. Was the man in command a Major Royce?''

"No, his nombre was Smeeth, I think. I had not seen him around town before. I know this Royce you speak of. He is muy malo. All our people are afraid of him.''

"That sounds reasonable. Did they say if they'd be coming back, or if?''

"Sí, mañana, after breakfast. Could you move your hand a little faster, por favor? I am starting to feel confused again down there.''

He didn't want to confuse her about the facts of life. So he mounted her properly and made her come the old-fashioned way. She said she was starting to get the hang of it now, and in fact seemed brave as hell tonight. So, knowing newcomers to sex are really curious about all the dirty stories as much or more than they're really in love, he spent an enjoyable few hours breaking the erstwhile virgin in. She said La Señora had already told her how to keep from getting in trouble, and that what she really wanted to learn was whether it was true a woman didn't feel she'd really possessed a man until he'd ejaculated in her all three ways.

Long before they ran out of steam, Lucrecia had possessed him completely and she said it made her feel very fulfilled as well as grateful. Then she told him she would love him forever and fell asleep. She was full of it, no doubt, and he felt sort of sorry for the next hombre the little monster he'd created decided to possess, unless the guy was in good shape.

He started feeling sort of sorry for himself, too, when he found out how loud Lucrecia snored. He consulted his watch, saw it was the wrong time to be doing anything but sleeping, but decided to give old Hector a shot, anyway. As he tiptoed past the lab door, the light was still on. He grinned, took a peep, and wished he hadn't. They'd gone out to the cages to get a tapir, and a tapir was a silly-looking beast even when it wasn't humping a naked woman. Gaston was on the chesterfield alone, reading a book. That seemed reasonable.

He moved without incident through the dark streets of Progreso with the machine gun action under one arm. At the herrera he found old Hector was still up. The blacksmith handed him a rod of almost perfectly round blue steel and asked him how he liked it. He said, "I like it a lot. How did you finish it so smoothly, viejo?"

Hector smiled modesly to reply, "With my hammer, of course. Rough hammer work is only for to look antique. A good smith can do anything with steel."

"Bueno. How much do I owe you?"

"Owe me? Do you mean I have worked half the night for to be *insulted*, Captain Gringo? How much do *I* owe *you*, for the honor of my grandchild, you stupid Yanqui?"

Captain Gringo apologized and took both the rod and the action to the machine shop on the quay. He still had a couple of hours before dawn and few businesses opened that early in any case. So he relit the lamp, cranked up the one-lung engine, and after experimenting with a switchboard put together by a mad scientist, had the machinery he needed at least hooked up.

Thanks to his own guestimate and old Hector's skill, the length of tough steel didn't need half as much work as he'd anticipated. He decided the few hammer marks that showed didn't matter and skipped turning it to a smaller diameter once he saw it would fit okay.

The length was more critical. He had to cut twice with the power saw and grind it to an even closer fit with a tool-sharpening wheel. That took a lot longer than threading both ends with the screw-cutting lathe. Then, for a few cursing minutes, it still didn't want to go. But with a little filing of the parts it was supposed to mesh with as well, he had the mechanism together just as the first light of dawn was streaming in the dusty windows. He turned everything off, put everything back as he'd found it, and let himself out. He still had to test-fire the gun before he'd know whether he'd done anything right, of course. But at least he had something to test now.

As he moved along the quay to avoid cutting through the same dangerous slum, a familiar figure reeled out of the cantina and hailed him. It was Turk Malone. The ex-boxer said, "I just got laid. Some guys are looking for you, kid."

"To lay me?"

"Naw, something about a patrol. Guy named Smith. Don't know him. He didn't come in with our bunch and I've never worked with him anywhere else. But he sure seemed anxious to find you"

"So I've heard. Where would Colonel Scroggs be, about now?"

"GHQ, at the Alcalde's old office, I guess. You wanna wake him up at *this* hour?"

"Don't want to. Ought to, though. A colonel should be less pissed-off than a general and I don't think Ramos knows what anyone else is doing, anyway, Scroggs would know, if anyone would, what this patrol is all about."

Turk shrugged and said, "Don't look at me. I gotta find a place to flop before I wind up in the bay. Jesus, don't never start the night with white rum and finish it with two colored gals in heat, kid."

Captain Gringo agreed never to try that and they parted friendly. He moved up a side street. He regretted it when a familiar figure fell in at his side from nowhere. But Paco Robles said, "Hey, amigo. I got something for to show you, eh?"

"What is it?" asked Captain Gringo cautiously, as the young tough reached inside his pants. But all Paco took out was a small shiny object, saying, "One of the girls lifted this last night, after we met you. We were having a party in the barrio for to celebrate making friends with you, see? These two cabrones came in, uninvited. We could do nothing much about it, because some of the older people were there and they always rat on us to the priest.''

Captain Gringo took the little gilt shield and held it up to the light. He said, ''Son of a bitch, this is a U.S. Secret Service badge! You say the guy carrying it crashed your party, Paco?''

''Sí, he was with a Mexican. *He* smelled like a cop, too. They said they came in with that last cargo from Los Estados Unidos Del Norte. Maybe they did. When they started asking questions about *you* and some Frenchman, I had one of the girls pick the Anglo's pocket. That is what she found. It was pinned to a wallet, of course, but the girl deserved something for her efforts, no?''

Captain Gringo said, ''I owe you, Paco. The SS has been after me for some time and anyone can see a town full of soldiers of fortune would be a good place to look. Did this Anglo go with a name?''

''If he gave his name, I did not hear it. Want me to ask around?''

''Gracias, no. I doubt he'd have given his right one anyway. Wait. If the girl got his wallet, there should have been some I.D. in it.''

Paco shook his head and said, ''There wasn't. He had mucho dinero and that badge attached to the one wallet. She said he had other stuff in the same pocket, but before she could get it all the dance was over and she slipped away before he could reach perhaps for a light. Do you wish for us to kill him, should we see him again, amigo?''

''No. He's just doing his job. You've done enough by tipping me off he's in town. You say he came in aboard a ship?''

''Not a ship, just a schooner, out of New Orleans with some big boxes for that crazy Cuban general. He gets lots of things from New Orleans. So for why does he take our food without paying for it, eh?''

''War is hell, Paco. Tell me something else. I've heard

there are Rurales camped out in the jungles around town. Know anything about it?"

Paco shook his head and said, "No. I heard some charcoal burners say they saw some Rurales out in the jungle. But I do not believe it. They may have seen banditos or smugglers. Rurales makes no sense."

"What does make sense to you, Paco?"

"I think that toad in Mexico City has sold us out to the Cubans, of course. Old Diaz would sell you his mother, cooked to your taste, so why should we be different, eh? If Los Rurales were out there, and meant to do anything about your crazy general, they would have hit you by now. Los Rurales are not sissies. There are not that many of you and, I mean no personal offense, the people here in town would stab you all in the back and shout Viva Diaz as Los Rurales rode in. So that is for why I do not think they mean to. Shit, I could raise a big enough gang for to take you out myself, if only we had the guns."

Captain Gringo thanked him for his words of cheer and went on back to the house. He found Lucrecia up, making breakfast, and the two lovebirds, or perhaps the two lovebirds and a herd of sex-mad beasts, still sleeping. So he'd assembled the Maxim and loaded it by the time Gaston wandered in, rubbing his eyes, and muttering, "Eh bien, whatever *you* were up to last night, I feel certain it was less disgusting. Have you ever tried to fornicate with a sow while a lady rode it bareback, kissing you fondly?"

"No, should I have?"

"I do not advise it. A lonely sheep herder may be one thing. But to fumble awkwardly with the family pets when one has a perfectly serviceable human pussy at hand, watching, just makes one feel très silly. Is that thing really ready to fire, Dick?"

"I don't know. I mean to burn away at least a belt to test it before I go up against anything that can shoot back."

It didn't work out that way. They'd just finished breakfast, alone, since Prunella seemed to want to sleep late for some reason, when the same two guys came pounding on the front door. Lucrecia let them in. The one calling himself Major Smith said, "The General's compliments, gentlemen, and he wants a well-armed combat patrol out to scout for those mysterious Rurales we keep hearing about."

Captain Gringo growled, "Well armed with what? I told General Ramos the only machine gun we have on hand came with its arming rod missing."

Smith shrugged and said, "I know. He told us. It can't be helped. If there's anybody out there, we're going to have to dig in. If it's just a rumor, that's one hell of a lot of work in this climate for nothing."

"I'd rather dig in anyway. I can't see the General with a pick and spade, but it's not as if we didn't have plenty of free labor. So far we haven't paid for one chicken here."

Smith smiled thinly and replied, "I pointed that out to his nibs. I agree he's not the greatest general I've ever served under. But he's the only one we've got. We've been paid to do as he says. So how soon can you guys be ready to go?"

Gaston asked what about a week from Tuesday. But Captain Gringo said, "May as well get it over with this morning, before the sun heats up. Who'll be going with us, you two?"

The delegation exchanged glances. Then Smith shrugged and said, "May as well. You'd better pick the others, Walker. We're new here. You'd know the best men to take along."

Captain Gringo nodded and said, "If any of them are sober. Meet us at GHQ in half an hour. That ought to give us time to round up a dozen or so good guys."

Smith frowned and asked, "Only a dozen? I was thinking along the lines of at least thirty or so. Full platoon strength."

"Did the General put you in command of the patrol, Smith?"

"No, but . . ."

"Half an hour, in front of GHQ. I'd rather take a few guys I know than stumble around in the woods with guys I don't. Some of the greener recruits might not know a bushmaster from a dry stick, and they run about even out there. By the way, do *you* know a bushmaster from a dry stick, and do you have a first name, Major?"

"They call me Soapy, back in the States. This is the Nogales Kid. What's the matter? Want to check our reps?"

Captain Gringo said, "The name Soapy Smith rings a bell. If Nogales Kid doesn't go with a knockaround guy, I don't know what would. Okay, like I said, half an hour, GHQ. We'll find out if you're any good or not. I'll watch out for Rurales. It's up to you to watch where you put your feet down in the jungle."

The men assembled in front of the Alcalde's office half an hour later looked more like a band of hoboes who'd just been thrown off a train than a combat patrol. Half of them were hung-over and none of them seemed too thrilled at the prospect of an early-morning romp through the woods. But they'd all been issued rifles, mostly Krags, and Ace Cavendish had even fitted his with a bayonet. He was a rather fragile looking guy who probably could use the edge. In addition to the gambler Captain Gringo had selected Turk Malone and the others he'd met on the boat coming up. Gaston had found a couple of rogues, as he called them, he'd served with before. One was a big black called 'Bama, and the other an ex-Legionnaire as old as Gaston but a lot bigger. He answered to Jacques. Smith and the Nogales Kid made up the rest of the party. Smith noted the Maxim on Captain Gringo's shoulder and asked, "How come? I though you said that thing was busted."

The taller American said, "I think it still is. But in a

pinch it can still fire single shots, and if it works on automatic, it could come in handy.''

"It looks awfully heavy, Walker.''

"It is. But you don't have to carry it. If the rest of you are paying any attention at all, let's get moving. We don't have to go through close order shit and read our general orders, do we?''

There was a murmur of laughter as Captain Gringo turned and just started walking. He didn't look back to see if anyone was following him. Professional soldiers would and he didn't want any other kind tagging along. They were on the outskirts of town in no time and as he led them along the clay road running through the corn and pepper milpas surrounding the community, he noted Turk and Tex Thatcher moving out on point without being told. He started to direct someone out as flank guards. Then he saw Rimfire was out to the right, ghosting through the tall corn with his Krag at port, while Bully Baker had taken left flank scout without having to be told. Soapy Smith caught up with Captain Gringo to say grudgingly, "You have these guys well trained, Walker.'' But Captain Gringo just shrugged and said, "You don't have to train good soldiers. And, no offense, but I just remembered that when I was chasing Apache with the old 10th Cav there was a con man and killer-for-hire fleecing marks up in Denver, Colorado. They called him Soapy Smith.''

Smith shrugged and said, "You got my number. I got run out of Denver by a spoilsport with a badge and a .44-40. Then I had to kill another gambler in Oregon, self-defense of course, and so I decided the States could manage without me for a while.''

"That sounds reasonable. What's the story on your pal, the Nogales Kid?''

"Not much different, except I'm white as the driven snow and old Nogales is half Papago. He's not as skilled with his hands as me. So he goes in more for simple stick-ups than the card or con games I'm more famous for. Are you writing a book or something, Walker?''

Captain Gringo nodded and said, ''Yeah, an Order of Battle for this outfit. I hope you won't take this unkindly, Major. But how in the hell did you get to be a major?''

Smith frowned and said, ''The Central Committee in New York commissioned me a major, of course. I told them I wasn't about to serve down here as a common soldier.''

Captain Gringo nodded grimly, and said, ''Right, you said you were a con artist and you'd play hell serving as a common soldier with your previous military experience. What brevet rank does Nogales hold with the Cuba Libres?''

''Oh, he's only a captain, like you.''

Captain Gringo didn't answer. The machine gun on his shoulder was getting heavy. So he shifted it to his left shoulder and adjusted the ammo belt running down from the breech and wrapped around his waist like a sash. He called back, ''Are you still there with the extra belts, Gaston?'' and the Frenchman replied, ''Oui, mais is this trip really necessaire? Regard the tree line ahead, Dick. A good place for an ambush, non?''

''If it wasn't there'd be no point in this recon patrol,'' said Captain Gringo. Then he raised his free hand, stopped, turned, and shouted, ''Okay, guys, spread out and form a line of skirmish at two-yard intervals on either side of this path. I'll keep the bee line with this Maxim and we regroup after we hull through the brush into the open rain forest beyond. Any questions?''

A distant voice replied plaintively, ''Is it too late to go on Sick Call, Captain?'' and Captain Gringo moved on. That wasn't a question, and the gag wore thin once you'd heard it a dozen times.

Soapy Smith asked nervously if there was anything he could do. Captain Gringo said, ''Yeah, hit the dirt and roll to the right if we come under fire. Gaston will be crawling up along my left with the extra ammo.''

He moved on another hundred yards and then, as they were getting within rifle range of the tree line, he swung the Maxim down to ride with its action braced against his right hip and its muzzle trained on the now not too distant wall of spinach beyond the last corn milpas. His men had by now spread out in a wide flanking front and weren't doing the corn a hell of a lot of good as they advanced in skirmish, their own gun muzzles aimed the same way.

As usual, in the tropics, the *edge* of the jungle grew more like greenhorns expected a jungle to grow. Underbrush that couldn't grow in the deep shade of more substantial trees or stand up to the machetes of the local farmers formed a hedgelike solid wall of tangled green. There were more species of plants in a single acre down here than one could classify in a whole New England forest. So whether one busted through without a machete depended a lot on just what in the hell was in the way. Supple gumbo limbo was slick barked and easy enough to bull through. Sea grape stems broke easily. But some of the crap seemed made of rubber tubing covered with broken glass. So as Captain Gringo made it to the tree line he slowed down to give everyone time to work through at the same pace. There was nothing interesting on the path ahead as he crouched in the shady arch of gum trees interlacing overhead. In the distance Turk Malone, who'd gone through with Tex—on point of course—stepped back on the path and signaled all clear. Captain Gringo shouted, ''Pick it up!'' and moved deeper into the jungle, which seemed more like the mouldy floor of a vast, pillared cathedral once the tangled edging was left behind. He glanced left and right to see others breaking through on either flank. Some idiot fired a gun and shouted, ''Snake! Snake!''

Some idiot always did.

Captain Gringo shouted, ''Keep it down to a fusilade, God damn it! Let them *guess* we're coming, shall we?''

He put the Maxim back on his shoulder and waved Turk

forward. They advanced into the jungle a little over a mile, his followers, save for the flank scouts, falling in behind him again to avoid walking in the slippery black muck of rotting leaves and mushrooms everywhere else. Then up ahead Turk stopped, turned, and signaled a question.

Captain Gringo halted the rest of the patrol and moved forward to see what was up. Smith and of course Gaston followed him to where Turk stood in the center of a big X formed by another trail crossing the one they were on at right angles. Turk asked, "Which way from here, kid?" and Captain Gringo reached for his pocket compass. But then Smith beat him to it with his own folded pocket map. Smith spread it open and said flatly, "To the right."

Captain Gringo frowned thoughtfully and said, "We can't be more than a mile or so from the Gulf, that way. Wouldn't it make more sense to take this other trail, inland? If it's part of a gum and charcoal gatherer's network surrounding the township, we may be able to circle Progreso completely before sunset, but—"

"General's orders," Smith cut in, adding, "We got a report there's a mysterious schooner ghosting around just offshore. The map says this path to the right leads to a cove deep enough for a shallow-draft sailing vessel. We'd better check that out before we look anywhere else, Walker."

"Oh? I thought I was leading this patrol. Correct me if I'm wrong."

"Well, I am a major, you know."

"Yeah, I know you let me shape it up and get it started for you because you couldn't drill a squad of rookies without them laughing at you, too. But okay, Major. You want us to go right, we'll go right. I just work here."

But as Captain Gringo waved the patrol toward the seacoast, Smith made no attempt to take full command. It figured. Political appointees were like that in every army. Why bother to bone up on tactical commands when there was always an NCO or junior officer who could give them for you? Smith was probably no worse than the so-called

Cuban general back in town. Maybe better. At least this shithead seemed willing to come along. General Ramos just sat on his fat ass and let the real soldiers worry about what they should do next.

Captain Gringo's guess about the lay of the land ahead was both right and wrong. They hadn't gone far when Turk stopped again with another questioning signal. When they moved forward to join him they saw they were indeed within sight of the Gulf, and in the distance a bare-poled lugger, not a schooner, lay at anchor in a sheltered cove. After that it got complicated. The ground around the cove had been cleared for a quarter mile inland. There were no houses or even shacks in view. That wasn't hard to figure. The cleared ground around the secluded cove was planted with pretty flowers: opium poppies. Mexico had no current laws against growing opium as a cash crop, but there was one hell of an export duty on all drugs leaving Mexico.

Captain Gringo told Smith, ''It's a smuggling operation. So what?''

''Don't you think we'd better investigate them fully?''

''Why? If there were any Rurales anywhere near here they'd have shot the shit out of that lugger by now. Evading export duties is a federal offense in Mexico or, come to think of it, anywhere else. On the other hand, if I was the skipper of a smuggling vessel, putting in where the local law shoots first and asks questions later, I'd have my crew armed to the teeth and keeping a sharp eye on the tree line all around. So what say we live and let live?''

Smith shook his head and said, ''General's orders. He'll expect a full report, Walker. We can't just *guess*. We have to *know!*''

''Jesue H. Christ, what's to know? Do you expect them to *tell* us anymore than we can figure out from here, Major? Those poppies are in bloom. So they have to be the new crop. That lugger's waiting for someone who collected the raw opium from the seed heads of the *last* crop to deliver. They wouldn't still be anchored there if they'd already picked up here. So about sunset, or maybe even sooner, a mess of local opium growers should be showing up around here, too, and guys who grow opium without bothering to tell their government about it tend to be truculent and well armed. The smartest thing we could do, right now, would be to head the other way, poco tiempo!''

Smith shook his head, took out a white pocket kerchief, and said, ''We'd better have a word with them, at least. If they are outlaws, the General may have use for that lugger.''

''You expect them to sell you a profitable smuggling operation for a flag wave? Forget it, Smith. Those guys won't want to go into the ferry boat trade. They're making more each voyage than the Cuba Libre Movement could afford for a whole fleet!''

But Smith had stepped out into the open and was waving the white kerchief wildly now. Captain Gringo cursed, turned to the others, and said, ''Stay here and cover us. Nobody's shot the asshole yet, but you never know.''

He moved out after Smith. Gaston followed with the extra ammo until Captain Gringo said, ''You'd better stay with the others. If this deal goes sour they'll need someone to get'em home safe.''

Turk Malone said, ''Gimme them spare belts, Frenchy.''

But the Nogales Kid said, ''My job, boys. I'm with Soapy, see?''

Nobody argued. So the three of them advanced down the path between the poppies, Smith in the lead, Captain Gringo in the middle with the Maxim, and the Nogales Kid bringing up the rear with an ammo belt. Gaston had refused to hand over more, saying, ''If it's a trap, none of you will last long enough to fire *one* belt, hein?''

As they approached the water, someone waved something white from the deck of the lugger and by the time they'd reached the beach of limestone pebbles a longboat was coming ashore. A man in the bows called out,

"How's it going, Masters?" and the man who'd said he was Soapy Smith called back, "Not too badly. The others were too coy, but this one's Richard Walker, the main one we want."

Captain Gringo had just digested this when the so-called Nogales Kid behind him said, "All right, Walker, drop that machine gun and stick'em-up. I've got you covered."

Captain Gringo did no such thing. He whirled, threw the heavy mass of steel in the Secret Service agent's face and as "Nogales" went down, firing the pistol in his hand at no place in particular, dove head first over him to land in the waist-high poppies, rolling, as he got out his own .38.

"Smith," on the path, made the awful mistake of standing still, fully erect, as he pegged pistol shots at waving poppies. He only got off three before the tree line in the distance blossomed a long line of gunsmoke and, though most of Captain Gringo's men missed at that range, some of them couldn't, and the real SS Agent Masters went down with a dozen or so .30-30 slugs in him.

Captain Gringo crawled back to the path where his Maxim lay atop the so-called Nogales Kid, who was breathing sort of funny through the smashed raspberry jam face he had left. Captain Gringo smashed his skull with the .38 to put him out of his misery. Then he put his pistol away and, still prone, swung the Maxim around atop the dead man's chest as, sure enough, the guys in the longboat had reversed oars and were on their way back to the lugger, firing wildly in the general direction of the shore-line.

Captain Gringo yanked the Maxim's arming lever, growling, "All right, I told Paco you guys were just doing your jobs, but enough of this shit. *I've* got a job to do, too!"

He opened up on the longboat, aiming of course at the water line, but since the men in the boat had at least their feet in the bottom of the boat, there was considerable howling as hot slugs and cooler jagged splinters tore through ankles, shins, and as the boat sank deeper, more important parts of human anatomy. As the longboat went under, a puff of oily black smoke rose above the lugger and they seemed to be weighing anchor as well. So Captain Gringo elevated his sights, reloaded with the belt "Nogales" had been kind enough to bring along, and proceeded to pepper the lugger with plunging fire.

Meanwhile Gaston and the others had gotten the range from the tree line and were putting telling shots into the same target. A machine gun fired six hundred rounds a minute. A repeating rifle could only get off about sixty in the same time, allowing for reloading with fresh clips. But when that many rifles were firing they added up to about the fire power of a second machine gun, so the guys on the lugger were in trouble and knew it. They couldn't get their anchor out of the mud with the exposed deck windlass. Their secret steam screw didn't have the power to drag it across the bottom. So they did the next best thing. They ran up a white flag.

Some of the soldiers of fortune in the distance ceased fire for some reason. But Captain Gringo growled, "Surely you jest," and put a long burst into their water line amidships. His followers took the hint and resumed fire. Captain Gringo wanted to, but he was running low on ammo, damn it.

Then Gaston joined him, after a long crawl through the poppies, muttering, "Merde alors. It serves you right for not listening to your elders."

Captain Gringo grinned and asked, "What kept you?" and took a fresh belt from the little Frenchman to reload and resume firing. It took a lot of small arms fire to sink even a wooden-hulled vessel of modest dimension. But they were getting there now. The lugger was listing shoreward as the sea bled into its hold through a multitude of mosquito bites and, better yet, the deck was now fully exposed. So nobody alive dared expose himself above it as the bodies on deck slid down into the scuppers, leaving long red streaks across the planking. Gaston asked mildly, "Are we not to give quarter to even their sea cook, Dick?" and Captain Gringo snarled, "What would we *do* with 'em? Oh, I forgot to tell you. It was a U.S. Secret Service ruse. They must have known a lot of guys wanted in the States would be here with the Cubans. Smith and Nogales were trying to take me aboard the easy way."

"Oui, so I assumed when they threw down on you. But if Tío Sam is secretly backing the Cuba Libre Movement..."

"That's what I just said. General Ramos would just have to let 'em go if we brought 'em in. So why bring 'em in?"

Gaston chuckled grimly and said, "It's going over, non?"

He was right. The lugger suddenly rolled bottoms up and, as muffled cries from inside rose beteen the bursts of gunfire, the whalelike bottom slowly submerged like, well, a whale.

Captain Gringo rose to his feet with the Maxim braced on his hip, feeling a little sicker than he let on, for he'd once worked for the U.S. Government, back in the dear dead days when he'd still thought the world was run on the level. But what the hell, their wives would get nice pensions and who wanted to be married to a fucking sneak, anyway? There were no heads bobbing in the harbor now. Guys bleeding good in tropic waters didn't last too long, anywhere, and the hammerheads of the Gulf were quicker to hit than most sharks. He swallowed the green taste in his mouth and muttered, "Okay, now let's get back on the job we were sent to do. We still have to find out why charcoal burners keep saying they've seen Rurales in the jungle."

Actually the uniformed men camped just off the main wagon trace between Progreso and the more important parts of Mexico were Federales, or Mexican Army, rather than Rurales, or Police Troopers. It didn't make much difference to Captain Gringo. The important thing was that Turk and Tex, out on point, spotted them first.

The Federales were enjoying La Siesta around a cook's fire, it being that late in the day by the time Captain Gringo's patrol moved in on them from the direction they weren't worried about. The troop of about a hundred and ten had been told to watch the main road and not let anyone go in or out of Progreso pending further orders from El Presidente. So though they had a road block posted on the wagon trace nearby, they made one big lovely target as they lounged about the fire enjoying their tortillas and coffee. It took Captain Gringo less than five minutes to explain his plan of attack and get his own men moving into position. He waited another five to make sure the guys he couldn't see were set up. Then he took a deep breath behind the mossy log he'd braced his Maxim across, aimed just to the right of the main clump of lounging Federales, and opened fire, traversing left.

The results were spectacular. Two thirds of the Federale troop were hashed before they could guess they were under fire. The riflemen to either side of Captain Gringo gleefully picked off the few he managed to miss as he hosed the whole camp with hot lead. And of course Jacques, 'Bama, and Bully Baker had meanwhile nailed the guards on the road block as soon as they'd heard the Maxim opening up.

One getaway man made it out the far side. There was always a man posted as getaway, with orders to run not walk as soon as contact with the enemy was made. But as Corporal Vallejo dashed through the trees, not sure what the hell had happened, but on his way to report it, Ace Cavendish stepped out from behind a tree to try out his new bayonet and his bayonet worked just swell. Ace braced his boot on the Federale to haul it out with a sickening suck as he told Rimfire, "Walker knows his stuff. The shit ran right into us just as Walker said he would.''

"Yeah, but, Jesus, did you have to take that chance, Ace? I'd have just shot the guy.''

"Have you no poetry in your soul, Rimfire? This is my third war and, so far, I'd never seen a guy bayonetted by anybody. I just wanted to try it, at least once.''

Then the mortally wounded but still alive Federale fired up from the ground with his pistol and Ace learned, the hard way, who so few people wanted to get close enough to an armed and well-trained soldier to bayonet him.

As Rimfire finished the dying but now grinning Federale off with his own rifle fire, Ace staggered over to a tree, tried to hold on to it, and muttered, "Aw, shit" before falling dead at its base.

But, thanks to Captain Gringo's planning, Ace Cavendish was the only casualty on his side. Los Federales had been wiped out to a man. Turk asked where next and Captain Gringo said, "Back to Progreso. We're running low on ammo, it's getting late, and sometimes it pays to get up from the table while you're ahead.''

"What about Ace?" someone asked. So Turk said, "What about him? He shouldn't have let hisself get killed and how long does anything last in this acid muck?''

But Captain Gringo shook his head and said, "We take him with us. I never leave my wounded and I carry my dead home when I can. This time we can. So that's what we'll do. Any objections?''

There were none and, in fact, some of the men were pleased to know that when and if they bought the farm under Captain Gringo he'd see they were buried instead of left to the flies.

They improvised a litter for their dead comrade by running gumbo limbo poles up inside his clothes and were soon on their way. As he strode beside Captain Gringo, carrying a lot less ammo now, Gaston said, "Dick, I have been thinking. I am, as you know, not unversed in the methods of the Mexican Army, since I fought on both sides during the Austrian Incident."

"So?"

"So something très curious is going on here. Those Federales, who no doubt deserved what they just got, were not behaving in the normal manner. The figures refuse to add up. Ramos has over a hundred of us holding Progreso, with more to come. But I doubt more than sixty or seventy of the so-called officers the Cubans have recruited so far are real fighters, and we have no troopers or privates at all!"

"I pointed that out to Ramos. I'm not sure he understood my point. If Los Federales were controlling that road back there they probably have other troops keeping an eye on the *other* ways in and out. So, yeah, we're surrounded by a superior force. So what?"

"Merde alors, what are they *doing* there, Dick? Why have they moved neither in or further back, if they are afraid of a handful of us?"

"That's easy. They have orders. They don't want either Spain or Spain's enemies sore at them. So officially nothing's going on in Progreso. At the same time, Mexico doesn't want a mess of professional gun-slicks getting practique ideas, like you, and going into business on their own. So Diaz is keeping us boxed in for Ramos, whether Ramos knows it or not. Probably not, since he's have hardly sent us out on a combat patrol if he was in friendly contact with Mexico City."

They trudged on in silence for a time. Then Gaston said, "Eh bien. Forget my practique suggestions regarding a romp in the woods to the border. We seem to be stuck with the invasion of Cuba after all. Mais let us reconsider what we just did back there, Dick. As I said, I was once an officer in the Mexican Army. If some cuchons had just shot the liver and lights out of a whole troop of mine, I would not like it at all and I assure you I have a sweeter disposition than your average Mexican officer, hein?"

"Yeah, we're going to have to get our guys dug in a little better, once we get back. We don't have to dig trenches around the whole town. Most of it's mad at us. I'll tell Ramos we'd better move to where we can watch the seaport and our backs at the same time."

"Sacre bleu, what do you mean you'll *tell* him, Dick? Ramos is a *general,* non?"

"Sure, on paper. But you know or I know he wouldn't make a pimple on a real lance corporal's ass. I think I can handle him. Ramos is an asshole, but even an asshole must want to live."

Apparently Ramos didn't. When they reported in he not only told them it was naughty to shoot up Mexican troops, but that he'd never ordered them out on patrol in the first damned place!

Colonel Scroggs and Major Royce were there on the dumber general's veranda to back him. So it had to be true. Captain Gringo started to ask, "Then why in the hell did that guy calling himself Smith say ... Never mind. Stupid question. But the guy sure had balls. Was he even one of us at all?"

Colonel Scroggs said, "He arrived yesterday afernoon aboard a smuggler we've been working with regularly. He had papers from the Cuba Libre leadership in New York that seemed in order. That's all I really know about him. You say he's dead?"

"Him, another SS man calling himself Nogales and, sorry guys, I think we sank your so-called smugglers, too. Obviously the Secret Service infiltrated the Cuba Libre Movement and they were playing a double game. Uncle Sam wants Cuba liberated. So they were running guns to you in an effort to make it easier. But Smith, at least, was more interested in picking up soldiers of fortune wanted by the U.S. Justice Department. So he acted cute and wound up dead. The hell with him. Do we have a secret agreement with Mexico, too, or is El Presidente just playing his own game by ear?''

General Ramos looked worried and said, ''I am not in direct touch with any Mexican authorities, although, of course, the central committee has assured me Mexico would not interfere as long as we caused them no trouble here.''

Major Royce said, ''You shouldn't have shot up that Federale troop, look you!'' But Captain Gringo just shrugged and said, ''Okay, we did. That was my fault. You guys have the entire native Mexican population pissed off at us. That's *not* my fault. Whether the Federales decide they've had enough of this shit when they find the remains of the troop my men and I just wiped out or whether some locals sneak out begging to be rescued along with their chickens, we have to face the fact there's a good chance the Mexican Army may take the gloves off and attack. I think we've got time to move the outfit to safer surroundings and dig in. If nobody misses that shot-up troop before sundown, and that's not far off, they won't know about it before morning. That gives us say fourteen or fifteen hours to make plans and we sure could use some good ones!''

The General looked like he was fixing to break down and cry. Scroggs said, ''See here, Yankee, *you* were the one who caused all the trouble in the first danged place. I've a good mind to turn you over to the Mexicans and have done with the problem!''

Captain Gringo didn't turn his head to look back at his men, still lounging around in the shade out front. He just asked softly, ''Do you think that's the most peaceful solution, Colonel?''

The Welshman, Royce, had been a real officer in a real army one time. So he stepped between them and said,

"We're all in the same pot together, look you! This is hardly the time to fight among ourselves."

Scroggs said, "Maybe not. But this infernal Yankee's the one who put us *in* the pot and, dang it, there just ain't time to dig in the whole outfit! Besides, we got more recruits and supplies coming in tonight and we just got to hang on to the port, dug in or no!"

Royce said, "I may have the solution, you see. Suppose Walker, here, were to dig in, away from the center of things?"

General Ramos bleated, "What about me and my Estralita?" So Royce said soothingly, "Neither you nor anyone on your general staff has done anything to make the Mexicans unhappy, sir. If they come at all they'll have orders to arrest the men who shot up their comrades, not staff officers of a friendly government, and the Cuban Government in exile *is* a friendly government, to both Diaz and his American backers, look you!"

The General still looked undecided. He probably had trouble deciding when to take a crap. But Colonel Scroggs nodded and said, "By gum, that ought to work. We got our commissions to show and we can back each other that Walker, here, never shot *anybody* at *our* command! How 'bout that, Walker? You reckon you and the boys who done the deed could hole up somewheres till the rest of us can calm them greasers down?"

Captain Gringo shrugged and said, "It looks like we'll *have* to, given so much backing by our superior officers."

Yucatan was pretty flat. But there was a gentle rise overlooking the unpopulated end of the harbor and, better yet, the one farm on the rise had a fresh water well. So Captain Gringo got his people around to it, carrying plenty of supplies and ammo, and told them to start digging in.

The subsoil was harder than marl and softer than granite, so the digging was tough, but then so would the walls of their trenches and spider traps be, so it evened out.

By sundown the men who'd been out on patrol were sweating like pigs and pretty well dug in. They were not alone. The general staff had made no effort to help, of course, but as word got around, other soldiers of fortune were joining them, armed with their weapons, packing their own supplies, and carrying any entrenching tools they could find. Some wanted to dig in with their adelitas as well, but Captain Gringo said it was to be a stag party. So though a few returned to town with their girls, most sent their adelitas packing. It was getting ominously obvious that something big was up and most of the knockaround guys recruited from all Latin America knew a lot more about Captain Gringo than the fat asshole who called himself a Cuban general. So by nightfall the rebel camp had split into two groups, the men with Captain Gringo and the boys with Ramos and his staff officers. That gave Captain Gringo almost a full company strength to work with and left the general staff with hardly enough flunkies to serve the drinks and shine the boots. They didn't like it much.

Captain Gringo had just set up his one machine gun, tripod and all, to cover the landward slope, when Colonel Scroggs and Royce came out from town to bitch about it. As they joined him on the hill Scroggs glanced around at the others in the gathering darkness and said, "See here, Walker. Your orders were to hole up with the men the greasers may want to hang, not the whole infernal outfit!"

Captain Gringo shrugged and said, "Mexico executes by firing squad, not hanging. I didn't ask these others to join us. They volunteered. If you don't want 'em up here with me, tell 'em."

Scroggs stuck out his chest, took a deep breath, and yelled, "All you men who weren't involved in that skirmish this afternoon, come back to town with me!"

Most of them didn't answer. A few chuckled dryly and a wiry tattood deserter from the Royal Navy called back, "Not bloody likely! When the Dons take to shooting lads with blue eyes, they don't aim careful enough for me, Colonel!"

There was a chorus of approval. Scroggs said, "Damn it, Walker, this is mutiny as well as misbehavior before the enemy!"

"What enemy? You said you could probably save your own asses by kissing theirs, Colonel. These guys, like me, don't like to trust themselves to the mercy of a piss-pot dictatorship. That's probably why we're all still alive. We mean to stay that way. So call it what you like, we're staying put until we see what Los Federales have to say about it!"

Scroggs might have huffed and puffed more. But Royce took his elbow and muttered something in his ear, and they moved back down the slope while they still could.

Someone on the hill struck a match to light a cook-fire in a trench. Captain Gringo called out, "No fires! We'll eat cold rations and make them guess where we are up here for now" He saw he had everyone's attention and added, "I don't know how long we may have to hold out here, or if we can. The Federales may not even come. If they do, they're only really after a few of us, remember. So if anyone has second thoughts, now's the time to think 'em! Once we're committed to battle up here, I have to tell you frankly I don't know how in the hell I can get you out of here alive!"

The husky black, 'Bama, chuckled deep in his throat and said, "You can't scare me, Cap'n. This chile' means to stay right here 'til them sassy Mexicans either whups his black ass or decides to leave it alone!"

Turk Malone said, "You're wasting your wind, kid. We all had the odds figured before we followed you up here. They're lousy. So what? There's no better place to run to and no better place to stand and fight. So get down off your fucking soap box and let's dig in some more!''

That was as good a suggestion as Captain Gringo could come up with. So he found a spade and started digging deeper behind his mounted Maxim. At his side, Gaston supervised, seated on the edge of the pit, and lit a claro casually before he said, ''Dick, I have been thinking.''

''You want to knock off the thinking and do some *digging*, damn it?''

''Mais non, I am a philosopher, not a gopher, and *someone* has to do some thinking around here right now. Has it crossed your adorable mind that we have been crossed double again, Dick?''

''Sure, Ramos and the other high-level Cuban officers have thrown us to the wolves. You just figured that out?''

''I don't think Ramos is a Cuban. I think he is Spanish. If Scroggs and Royce were not Spanish agents as well, they would be helping us dig in, non?''

Captain Gringo started to tell him he was nuts. Then he rested on his spade and said, ''Hmm, real soldiers of fortune would be sort of dumb to take their chances with pissed-off Mexican Federales, and it was Royce who came up with this grand suggestion. But, Jesue, talk about wheels within wheels!''

Gaston took a drag on his cigar and said, ''Butcher Weyler is said to be a devious person, non? Consider what he has just accomplished here, by infiltrating the Cuba Libre Movement with a mere handful of big fibbers. The kingpin must be Ramos, of course. The central committee in New York would not have put him in charge had he spoken as stupidly to *them*. Ergo the stupid act is just an act. He is really working for the Spanish forces in Cuba. He probably commissioned Scroggs and Royce, along with other key officers, himself. The Bedouin say that once a camel has its nose in one's tent, the rest comes easily enough, hein?''

''Okay, so Ramos could be a Spanish spy. That would

explain a lot. But what would be the *point* of all this bullshit if . . . Oh boy, never mind, I see it all now!''

But Gaston explained it anyway, saying, "Oui, as a double agent Ramos has been taking money raised by the Cuba Libre cause to gather all the professional soldiers who might manage a successful invasion of Cuba here in Mexico, where they *can't*. By deliberately allowing his forces to run wild and annoy the local Mexican population, he has also assured Spain the men they fear may not be long for this world. One must admire a devil like Butcher Weyler. Those new things he calls concentration camps, whatever they may be, are the least of his inventions. He has how you say suckered Mexico into wiping out the best fighters Cuba can possibly recruit, non?''

"No. He hasn't wiped us out yet."

"True, but then, the night is still young."

Though a full tropic moon was rising too big and bright to look real the western slopes of the hill were black as a tax collector's soul. So Paco Robles was able to work his way too close for comfort before he was challenged and identified himself as a pal of Captain Gringo's. The tall American had no use for unarmed kid recruits. But he and Gaston crossed over anyway to hear what the gossip in town was at the moment.

As Captain Gringo waved him in and offered him a smoke, the young tough asked him instead what the hell was going on. Paco said, "We heard the Cubans had split into two camps. If you are with this bunch, amigo mio, these must be the good guys. If me and my gang had guns we would join you. Hey, you got guns for us, amigo?''

Captain Gringo started to say no. Then he called 'Bama over and said, "No offense, 'Bama, but you speak good Spanish and look more like a native than the rest of us, so

I've got a job for you. Do you think you could find that shot-up Federale camp in the dark?''

'Bama nodded and said, "Sure, Cap'n. But then what?''

"I'd like you to guide this guy and his gang there to salvage their weapons. Once they're armed they'll still need an old pro to show 'em how it's done.''

"How *what's* done, and what if the fool Mexicans have already *found* them Federales we wiped out, Cap'n?''

"That makes two reasons to pick you for the job, 'Bama. If you can arm and lead a guerilla band those double-crossing Spanish agents won't be expecting, playing it by ear, so much the better. If the deal goes sour, one local Negro running with a bunch of unarmed locals should be easy enough to sell. Let's see if we can dope out a good sales pitch if you guys run into anybody bigger than you.''

He turned to Paco and said, "We stumbled over an opium crop out of town a ways today, amigo. Know who owns it?''

"Sí, my Tío Luis, for one. We heard about you guys shooting up those smugglers. None of *us* were working with the pobrecitos. For why were they putting in there when the crop was nowhere near ready for harvest?''

"They were after something else. Here's your story. You heard there was a shipwreck or something. So you and your gang are going out to see if there's any salvage. You don't know shit about the opium. Why would *you* be interested in poppies in bloom if you did? Any army guys or lawmen you meet are welcome to come along and see if anything interesting has washed up on the beach, see? Naturally, they'll tell you they're on duty and that you kids shouldn't be out so late at night. They'll want to get rid of you without making any noise so that *they* can salvage the wreck without pestering their officers about it.''

Paco grinned in the moonlight and said, "That's for sure! You are one sneaky devil, Captain Gringo! I am glad we are on the same side. Oh, by the way, a puta who says *she* is on your side as well is waiting down the slope for to see you. Shall I call her in, now?''

Captain Gringo shook his head and said, ''I need a cunt up here right now like I need an even bigger hole in my head. Tell old Lucrecia to just burn a candle in her window or something for now.''

Paco said, ''Her name is not Lucrecia. It is Esperanza, I think she said.''

Captain Gringo blinked and asked, ''Esperanza? Big Basque brunette?''

''Sí, too big for me, or even you, if you know what is good for you. Not bad looking, but Jesus, the *fists* on that muchacha! You want for us to get rid of her?''

Captain Gringo shook his head and called out, ''Esperanza, up here, on the double, you crazy little broad!''

So a few moments later a lady who could hardly qualify as little had joined them on the crest and was kissing Captain Gringo wetly as she tried to crack his ribs. She was dressed in a striped seaman's jersey and canvas pants. She could still grip pretty good with her vaginal lips as she pressed her pelvis against his. When they came up for air, he laughed and said, ''First things first. 'Bama, Paco, get going. If you get to the guns, work back and lay low 'til the shooting starts. Then see who's shooting at us and act accordingly. If it's the two-timing general's guys, hit 'em from the rear and dirty. If it's the Mexican Army or Rurales, skip it. We don't want the local population massacred, no matter how we save our own tails.''

'Bama asked, ''What if you guys up here cain't *save* your own tails, Cap'n?''

''It's been nice knowing you. You can probably get a job picking bananas or something until the heat blows over and a costal trader blows in. Get going and good luck, guys.''

'Bama and Paco nodded and vanished down the dark slope as Captain Gringo led his old gunrunning girlfriend over to his machine gun emplacement. Some of the others started to follow, until Gaston stopped them, asking them if they were writing a book or something, so Captain Gringo and Esperanza were soon cuddled cozy in his gun pit. But when she put his free hand against her own love pit he said, "Not now, damn it. Is your schooner in the harbor, honey?"

"Hell, no, I walk on water like Jesus. *La Nombre Nada* is moored out in the roads. I rowed ashore for to see if the coast was clear before I landed the ammo I carry for the Cuba Libre Movement. A Cuban officer who met me on the quay said it was. But when you have been in the business as long as me you develop a sixth sense. I sent my longboat back for to start bringing in the shells. But in the confusion I slipped away for to see what I could see, and a lady who sells other services to soldados put me on to that sweet young boy. So the rest you know, eh? For why can't we tear off a quickie, here in the shadows? None of your men are watching and I don't think anyone else will be coming this way for a while."

"I don't want to be caught with your pants down if you're wrong. What was that about *shells!* Ramos doesn't have any big guns, honey."

But she said, "Sure he does. I delivered them myself, last trip. A pair of French 75s. They were a bitch to get ashore, too. You mean you did not *know* this, Dick?"

"I don't think I was supposed to. Tell me, did you deliver more than one machine gun, or did anyone you know of?"

She snuggled closer and started fumbling with his fly as she replied, "We landed, oh, four Maxims and a Belgian Browning, trip before last, why?"

"Oh boy! I was cussing Woodbine Arms instead of the prick who got to the crate ahead of me, too! I see it now. They had to issue at least one machine gun to a known machine gun expert. But they didn't want me smoking anyone up with it, so they removed the arming rod. What a sweet bunch of guys!"

He held Esperanza's wrist to keep her from jerking him off as he brought her up to date on his misadventures. Esperanza had been in the business longer than he had. So she could add things up pretty good in her head, too. She said, "Ramos lied when he said he had not given those Secret Service men authority for to lead a patrol out and into the trap they'd set up for you, of course. Not even a crazy lawman would have had the balls to pull that on his own. Too many things could hae gone wrong if the headquarters staff hadn't known about it."

"Tell me something I don't know. The question is whether the U.S. Secret Service thought they were working with real Cubans or Spanish double agents."

"That's easy. Nobody working for Tío Sam would have trusted any of Butcher Weyler's hombres. Weyler even has the *Spanish* nervous and they are trying for to get up the nerve to recall him as governor. His men down there in Progreso must have simply duped your Smith and Nogales."

"Yeah, meaning Tío Sam is going to be mad as hell at the Cuba Libre Movement, not Spain, when he misses them terribly! Jesus H. Christ, talk about two birds with one stone! Gaston's right. That Weyler bastard is *sneaky!*"

She said, "Bueno. Why don't we just sneak down the dark slope before the moon rises high enough for to light it up and make mad gypsy love in my stateroom as *La Nombre Nada* sails out of the harbor? They can't know I suspect anything, no gunboats will be off the bar before the midnight tide and—"

"How many guys can you load aboard *La Nobre Nada?*" he cut in, adding, "I've close to seventy-five or eighty up here."

She shook her head and said, "Too many, Dick. We could load them in the hold like slaves, once we unlade. But there is not enough food and water to last that many hombres to the next safe port of call and, if there was, do you really *want* those cabrones to have the cargo the Cubans paid for? I told my bos'n to take it easy, bringing the stuff ashore by lighter with the tide out . So if we leave right now we can keep them from getting at least a third of it, no?''

''No. There has to be a better way. I can't abandon my own people. I can't leave the townspeople to the mercy of a gang who takes orders from a prick called Butcher, and though I'm not a fan of El Presidente Diaz or even Tío Sam these days, I can't leave them with the impression they've been double-crossed by the real Cuban rebels.'' He thought, and added, ''I can't occuppy this hill much longer, either, if Ramos has *artillery* I didn't know about. That was real cute. I thought they just wanted us out of the way. But that's not the plan. They wanted us all up here in a bunch, as an easy artillery target!''

He raised his voice and called Gaston over. The little Frenchman joined them, saying, ''Mon Dieu, you children still have your clothes on? What is up, aside from your adorable pants, I mean.''

Captain Gringo filled him in quickly, then said, ''You're the old field artillery man here, Gaston. How long do you think we have?''

Gaston said, ''They won't want to open up until *La Nombre Nada* finishes unloading and sails merrily away, lest news get about that the private army Cuba is paying for seems to be blowing itself to bits for some reason with ordnance from the same source. But may I suggest we get the fuck off this crest before the moon rises much higher? Once it's overhead, with all the slopes lit up—''

''Hold the thought,'' Captain Gringo cut in, asking Esperanza, ''Can you signal your crew aboard your schooner from up here, doll?'' and she said, ''Sure. How did you suppose smugglers work at night? All I need is a steady light for to move my hand back and forth across.''

That was easy to arrange. So in no time Esperanza was sending the dots and dashes Captain Gringo dictated to her, using nothing more than her big right hand and a little improvised torch. Somewhere out on the water a firefly seemed to be winking back at them. Esperanza said, "Bueno, and I don't think anyone on the quay saw either signal. If they did, they couldn't have read it. International Morse is not for serious business. *La Nombre Nada* will speed up the delivery, put out to sea, then wait for us in another cove I know of to the east. It's about ten kilometers, though. So if you do not wish for to be spotted in the cold gray dawn . . ."

Captain Gringo didn't. So he stood up and called out, "Everyone but the lookouts, front and center. We've got to make some other plans, poco tiempo, before this position gets the shit blown out of it!"

Down on the quay, the Spanish Secret Agents Scroggs and Royce were pleased at the way the supplies were coming ashore. General Ramos, of course, was up in his quarters with his Spanish mistress and if she wasn't pleased by the way he was eating her she was at least being a good sport about it. Butcher Weyler paid her well to keep an eye on his other spies, just in case.

Neither Scroggs nor Royce had spotted the screened signal from the schooner moored out in deeper water, of course. But Scroggs had seen Esperanza's signal and was still bitching about what it could have meant. Royce told him, "It doesn't matter, look you. They may have a few friends left behind our lines. But what of it? We know all the real fighting men our side was worried about have dug in up there and, ah, one of them seems to be cooking in his fox hole now. As soon as we get rid of that schooner we'll just wheel out the ordnance and blow the blighters to bits. If any word at all gets out we can blame it on the Mexicans, assure the fools sending all their goodies here instead of Cuba it was all Captain Gringo's fault, and with any luck at all, get them to send us more supplies and suckers, you see!''

Scroggs said, ''I still wish I knew how many supporters they have here in town. These greasers would stab a man in the back for his shoes and we know they're pissed at us.''

Royce chuckled and said, ''With good reason. That was part of the plan, too. Thanks to our own picked men behaving most unprofessionally the professional soldiers the Cubans have been trying to recruit won't be missed by anyone. Heads up, Esperanza's bos'n seems to have something to tell us.''

The bos'n did. He came over to report, ''The last case of shells is ashore and since your employers paid us in advance, our skipper says it's time to go home, eh?''

Royce said, ''Bueno, don't let us stop you. But where is Esperanza, anyway? I haven't seen her for some time.''

The bos'n shrugged and replied, ''That is because she has been out on *La Nombre Nada,* lying down in her stateroom for some time. She says she does not feel good. Don't ask me why. She *hits* when one asks her if she is having her period.''

Royce chuckled and said some women were like that at certain times. The bos'n got them to sign a receipt, turned away, and a few minutes later he was bobbing out to *La Nombre Nada* in the longboat cum lighter. Scroggs said, ''That's that. Let's get out the 75s and load 'em up.''

''Don't you think we'd better wait until that schooner's out of sight, Colonel?''

''It's already hard to see, so they can't see shit from out there. I want the guns in place before the moon rises high enough to pin them down up there. I'll round up the gun crews. You just get your guys to work on them shells, old son. We promised the General we'd finish the job early enough for him and his gal to get some sleep after midnight. So let's get cracking.''

They did. The so-called soldiers of fortune who hadn't

joined Captain Gringo and Gaston on the hill outside of town were fewer in number, but all well trained, by the Spanish Army. So in less than an hour they'd wheeled the two field pieces real soldiers of fortune weren't supposed to know about out of a certain waterfront warehouse and down to the far end of the paved quay. Scroggs had his five-man gun crews, ten men in all, dig the guns in and sandbag them in the softer beach beyond, with their muzzles trained on the not too distant hilltop. By this time Royce and his own crew of carefully picked cutthroats had hauled enough ammo for a small war up the quay as well.

Scroggs stared seaward and said, "I don't see that schooner, now." But Royce said, "Give Esperanza more time. The rumble of gunfire carries for miles over water at night. Besides, I have to get my machine guns around to the far side and that may take a while, look you. We'll have to machete our way well wide of Walker's observation posts up there, now that the moon's up. We'd better synchronize our watches. I have nine forty-eight. You?"

"Close enough. I'll give you until ten-thirty. Then I'll open fire. We *have* to finish them off ourselves before those Spanish ships come in at midnight, flying the Cuban rebel colors, if we don't want the Dons claiming that bonus on Captain Gringo and the frog."

Royce lowered his voice to whisper, "Watch it. A couple of our so-called privates are Spanish junior officers. One of them was just asking me why we were going to so much trouble instead of just waiting for the big kiss-off."

Scroggs snorted in disgust and muttered, "Lazy bastards. It's no wonder Spain needs help with her rebels. But old Weyler's posted a standing reward on Walker in particular and I ain't about to share it with no Spanish commodore. So get moving, Royce. We don't want our reward money slippin' down the fur side of yon slope once I opens up, hear?"

Royce nodded, called to his own crew, and vanished into the darkness. The next forty-five minutes felt like a million years to Scroggs as he paced up and down behind his gun crews, smoking nervously.

Then at last it was ten-thirty. So Colonel Scroggs tossed his cigar away, put his hands to his ears, and shouted, "Gun number one, fire one for range!"

The French 75 cleared its throat with a flaming roar, and the first shell landed a little short, but sure blew a hell of a hole out of the moonlit hillside. Scroggs shouted, "Elevate three clicks and . . . fire!" Then, when he saw the top of the hill illuminated from behind in an orange glare, he yelled, "Depress one click and . . . fire!"

The shell landed smack in the center of Captain Gringo's hilltop position. So Scroggs laughed and told the other gun crew, "Go thou and do likewise! We got the rascals ranged, boys. So let's jus' keep up the good work 'til we run 'em down the fur side into Major Royce's machine gun nests!"

The twin 75s proceeded to do just that, lobbing shell after shell into the positions atop the hill, unaware they were empty and had been for some time. In the nearby darkness, crouched behind a low but sea-grape-covered dune, Gaston asked Captain Gringo, "Eh bien, have you not heard enough, Dick? The cochons are burning a lot of ammo *we* might be able to use, non?"

Captain Gringo nodded and said, "When you're right you're right. Esperanza, keep your ass down. The rest of you take your dress on me and don't anybody get out ahead of the same!"

Then he snicked the Maxim braced across the dune ahead of him off safety and simply opened fire. The results were dramatic as well as gratifying. Scorggs hadn't thought to post any back-up. So he and his gun crews went down like pins in a bowling alley as Captain Gringo hosed them good. Then he paused, ears ringing, to tell Gaston, "Give me another belt, damn it!"

Gaston reloaded for him, but said, "No more, dammit

yourself, my noisy child. If one of those shells took a round with its fuse—"

"Okay, let's see what we got, then," Captain Gringo cut in, adding, "You stay here with Esperanza and this Maxim. It's the only one we got and Royce may be coming back with more if he heard us just now!"

Then he rose, drew his .38, and moved in with Turk and Tex close behind, covering him. He rolled over the first body with his foot. Nothing. When a guy takes eight rounds of .30-30 he seldom has much to say. But Scroggs was still alive, just, and as Captain Gringo stood over him, pointing a thoughtful .38 at his head, Scroggs moaned and said, "Hold it, old son, mayhaps we can still make a deal."

"From the bottom of the deck again? No thanks, Colonel. I hope you won't take this personal, but I've shot army mules I was fonder of and your razzle dazzle cost me a good man this afternoon."

"Hold on, Walker! Don't shoot me! I know something you don't know!"

"I'm listening."

"Do I have your word you won't finish me off, if I tell you a tale that could save your ass?"

"You have my word. But only if it's good."

"It is! I can see you've grasped what's been goin' on hereabouts, so I won't waste time about that. But tonight's the night of the big kiss-off, see? The Dons know the rug's worn thin here in Progreso. So Weyler plans to pull his own people out. Only, afore they go, the ships flying rebel flags mean to bombard the shit outten this whole town!"

"What the hell for? Oh, right, first Cuban rebels shoot up a Mexican army unit and then they shoot up a Mexican town and if Mexico's still shouting Cuba Libre after that, Diaz sure must need Yankee money bad! Did you guys figure we'd turn the tables on those Secret Service guys you were working with, as Cuban rebels, they thought?"

"Sure. That was Royce's notion. He was betting on

you. I'll tell you true the rest of us didn't really give a shit. But you're still alive, I've warnt you to get goin' afore the Spanish fleet steams in, and you gave me your word. So I sure could use a doc about now!''

Captain Gringo nodded and told Turk Malone to take care of him. Turk shrugged, aimed his rifle, and blew the bastard's brains out, saying, ''*I* never gave the mother-fucker *my* word, and old Ace was a good kid, kid.''

''I noticed. Okay, we'd better put our heads together with Gaston, now that we've some idea what's going on.''

Back atop the dune, Gaston's first suggestion, of course, was that they all run like hell for the cove *La Nombre Nada* would be waiting for them in for at least a little while.

Captain Gringo shook his head and said, ''No, for a lot of reasons, Royce is between us and the schooner with a lot more fire power than we can carry. Those heavy guns can't follow us through jungle like pups. The schooner's in danger, too, if a Spanish fleet with its gloves off is coming this way. The pricks are even flying Cuban colors. So Esperanza's crew could wind up dead before they knew what hit 'em! There's only one answer. You're not going to like it. I don't like it much, either. We send Esperanza around through the jungle, mounted, with a mounted escort, to tip off her crew if the rest of the plan won't work.''

Esperanza said flatly, ''I'm staying here. What's the plan, lover?''

He said, ''The Spanish fleet's coming in with the next tide. They want the locals to remember them fondly as the Cuban rebels they're already pissed at. So they'll move in close enough for their false colors to show by the rocket's red glare and all that shit. They won't expect any heavy fire in return. They know those 75s over there are the only ordinance on shore and, and who's going to tell them their own side doesn't own it anymore?''

Gaston cackled with glee and said, ''I will! There is

plenty of time to swing them about and dig them in again!
Leave it to me!''

"I'm going to have to. I have to cover your ass with the
one machine gun we've got and hope that jury-rigged
action holds up a little longer. Turk, I've got a detail for
you, too. We know where Scroggs and his bunch are. We
know where Royce and company is supposed to be. That
leaves Ramos and the general staff. Can do?''

"Sure. Can I lay that dame before we shoot her? She's
some dish.''

"I want her and the General taken alive. I mean it,
Turk. You can screw or shoot the rest of his GHQ staff if
you like, but I want to turn Ramos and his hopefully
hysterical muchacha over to the alcalde or, better yet, the
local priest, as political refugees. Can you guess why?''

Turk grinned and said, "Jesus, you play chess as good
as Weyler, don't you? If Ramos and the dame ever expect
go get back to Spain, they'll have to tell the Mexican
government they're Spanish, right?''

"Why do you tell me how my own cards read, Turk?
Get going, and watch out for Welshmen with machine guns.
He's still the wild card in the deck.''

Turk barked out eight names, told them they'd just
volunteered, and led them away in the darkness. Captain
Gringo asked Gaston what he was waiting for, picked up
the Maxim, and told Esperanza she got to carry the spare
ammo for being so stubborn. So five minutes later they
were up on the flat roof of a waterfront shop, closed for
the night, with a nice field of fire, and Esperanza was
taking off her clothes for some reason.

He laughed and said, "Gee, bare tits look grand in the
moonlight, doll. But, no kidding, this is neither the time
nor the place. This gravel roof would tear hell out of my
knees, if not your tough ass, and I can't shoot for shit
while I'm tearing off a piece. I tried it once. So I know.

Esperanza said, "Pooh, if those others were coming
back, they'd have gotten here by now, no?''

He frowned thoughtfully and said, "Yeah, I wonder what Royce is up to. Even if he didn't hear another machine gun in the distance he must have noticed by now that nobody's shelling the positions we deserted just in time. Welshmen sure can act spooky. So leave my damned fly alone, damn it!"

"I just wish for to kiss it, to see if it still likes me, querido."

"I know what you're trying to do. So cut it out. I'm not going to lay you until I make sure you'll live long enough to enjoy it. I mean it, Esperanza!"

She sat pouting with her naked spine against the roof parapet and told him he was either a sissy or that he'd been cheating on her a lot of late. Esperanza was like that. They ran into one another every six months or so and every time they did she acted like they were going steady. He knew better than to ask the big Basque broad who'd been in *her* pants since the last time they'd slept together. Women fibbed enough to him as it was. But as the moon rose ever higher and nothing much else seemed to be going on, it was getting harder and harder. Harder to resist Esperanza's literally open invitation, too. The way she was sitting there stark naked in the moonlight with her knees not at all close together was doing awful things to his glands. But a soldier on guard wasn't even supposed to read. So he hung tough and waited, and waited, while nothing around them moved in the moonlight except Esperanza's hand. He asked, "Do you have to do that, doll?" and she replied demurely, "Somebody has to, if you won't. I told you the last time I am forced to masturbate at sea because it is not seemly for the skipper to screw her crew, no?"

Actually, it would have been safe for Captain Gringo to help his old pal out, had he known what was going on on the far side of his old positions. Royce and his own machine gun sections had naturally been puzzled when the barrage had lasted such a short time. So Royce had sent a runner to ask Scroggs why. The runner hadn't come back. So Royce had sent another, then another. When all three failed to come back with any answer at all, Royce had seen the light. He'd warned his men to keep a sharp look-out as he led them cautiously back toward town. So once they were single file on the moonlit path, guns over shoulders, 'Bama had shouted, "Now! Hit 'em in the cajones, muchachos!" and Paco and his gang, now armed with Mexican Army rifles, had done just that.

Unlike Scroggs, Royce had been shot dead in the short furious fusillade of flanking fire. So when one of the Mexicans whose sister had been raped found the Welshman's body, he had to content himself with just cutting its cock and balls off.

It took 'Bama a while longer to reform the disorganized guerrillas. They were ladrones first and guerrillas second, and a guy who shoots a guy with boots on deserves new boots, no? But in less than an hour 'Bama had them coming 'round the mountain and almost got them shot when he shouted "Take cover!" instead of answering Captain Gringo's rooftop challenge sensibly.

Fortunately they recognized each other's voices. Captain Gringo shouted, "Report!" and the big black shouted back, "Ain't nobody left but us chickens, Cap'n! For raw recruits these boys did right well. We got you some more machine guns, could you use 'em!"

"Just leave one down there for me and I'll come down and get it. Any prisoners, 'Bama?"

"Now why would a man as smart as you ask a question like that, Cap'n? These old Mex boys was at family feud, not war, if you follows my drift. I'll bring this gun up to you, right?"

"Wrong. I'm not the only guy around here asking dumb questions. Get over to Gaston and the others at the end of the quay. He'll fill you in on what's up."

As they left, Esperanza asked how he felt about getting it up now. He chuckled, told her it had been up for some time, but they still had other things to worry about. But then Turk Malone and his gang appeared below. Turk stiffened when Captain Gringo called down to him. Then said, "Oh, it's you, kid. How come you left your Maxim down here leaning against the wall?"

"Never mind. How did it go at the general's, Turk?"

Malone laughed and said, "They was going sixty-nine when we busted in on 'em. The gal covered her tits and started screaming right off she was a Spanish citizen. We let 'em plead sanctuary at the church across the way. I don't think the Mex padre wanted to give it to 'em much. But he did. So about now they should be blabbing to some mighty interested Mexican priests. The General got sort of hysterical, too, once he seen the bodies downstairs."

"They were going at it hot and heavy and never heard the shots?"

"What shots, kid? Knives are better for work in the dark. Where do you want us to hit next?"

Captain Gringo sent Turk and his men to join Gaston, too. Then he turned to Esperanza and said, "Okay, doll, you've been begging for it and now you're gonna get it!"

"Wait, let me put my canvas pants under my bare rump, first."

"Bullshit. I need 'em for my knees. Nothing else we've got up here is heavy enough to stand up to the wear and tear."

Actually, he was just kidding and it wasn't bad, screwing in the moonlight atop all their clothes. He'd forgotten how tight Esperanza was, despite her size. She said she'd forgotten how big he was, too. They always bullshitted one another at times like these. But they both enjoyed their first mutual orgasm immensely, after having to wait so long, and when Esperanza begged to get on top he let her. But they were just getting it right that way, when all hell started breaking loose. Captain Gringo stared up at Esperanza, outlined against an orange sky, and said, "Hold the thought for later, doll! Nobody comes that hard. Gaston's got both 75s going, and somebody's firing back!"

So they both got dressed and stood on the roof to watch the fireworks. By the time it was over half the town was watching from other rooftops all around, so nobody paid any attention to the unusually tall couple above an empty store as the whole harbor glowed orange save for the black outlines of five vessels standing just offshore, winking like big floating fireflies as Gaston lobbed shells at them from shore. Some few of the bright flashes out there were from big guns firing in reply, not too well aimed. Others were the explosions of Gaston's well-placed shells. He sent up a mighty column of water now and again, of course. But most of his rounds went where Gaston aimed them, and Gaston was only bragging a little when he said he could drop a shell in a barrel from three miles away. The Spanish vessels were more like a quarter mile out. You could see their false Cuban colors from shore when a shell flashed nearby. It must have occurred to at least one Spanish skipper that the Cuban banner was causing him more trouble than it was supposed to. So he lowered it and ran up the red and gold of Imperial Spain, with a spotlight trained on it. That gave Gaston a swell target. The skipper on the bridge must have wondered why Mexico was mad at everyone tonight, when a 75 landed smack on the bridge of his already badly listing vessel.

None of the ships were ironclads, since everyone knew the Cuba Libre Movement had no real navy. So none of them stood a chance when a 75 was pounding them. Another sinking Spaniard raised a white flag. But the townspeople standing around Gaston's sweating gun crews to cheer them on shouted, "Sink them! Sink them! They just blew up the bakery and this is not time to show quarter!"

So Gaston bowed to the crowd, traversed one gun, and finished it off with another two shells. Everyone applauded, so he drew a bead on the bastard steaming seaward, full speed. His round exploded on the fan deck, but the steamer kept going to either sink out on deep water or report back to Butcher Weyler that something had gone terribly wrong with his clever plans tonight. But four out of five wasn't bad. As the glow died down, a lot of heads were bobbing out there in the water now. Those who had any sense would swim for Cuba. Because Paco Robles and his muchachos were not the only highly pissed off Mexicans who were waiting on shore with guns, machetes, or anything else they could get their hands on.

On the distant rooftop, Captain Gringo turned to Esperanza and said, "Well, sometimes you gotta win. It's the law of averages, see?"

She said, "Sí, could we find a more comfortable place for to fuck some more, querido?"

He didn't think Lucrecia or even old Prunella would understand if he took her there. So he said, "If we start now, we can make it to your schooner by morning. We'll take Gaston, Turk, some of the other guys really wanted bad here in Mexico. The others should be able to stay here long enough to catch another boat out. I imagine they'll find themselves pretty popular here now, as a matter of fact."

"Whatever you say, querido mio, as long as you screw me good, at least once, before we start hiking. Once we are on the trail with others, we won't be able for to make love for hours and, oh, Deek, I wish to make love to you so mucho!"

He kissed her fondly and said, "There's no hurry now. I'm sure we can work something out, doll box."